EMERGENCY!
10-33 on channel 11!

When a violent summer storm hit Rodgersville, its residents were prepared for the
all-too-frequent disruption of electric and
telephone service. But Ronnie and David
Winthrop, off in the fields to round up the
horses, were not prepared to hear the frantic message over their walkie-talkies:
Emergency! 10-33 on Channel 11!

Young Jane Horton, trapped in her family's overturned camper, her mother and
father hurt and unconscious, had only one
hope of rescue—the newly installed Citizens Band radio in their truck. Pinned
down in the wreck, Jane sent out her ter-
rifying call, praying to be heard.

Thus begins this fast-paced adventure
story that races to its climax as the two
boys, and their friend Mary Lou (Handle:
Bluebird), create a network of CB volunteers to find Jane and her family before
the river floods over. For then, the search
through the many small roads and paths
would be impossible. And every second
counted in the lives of the Hortons.

So, too, begins the adventure of Ronnie
Winthrop, eager to be first to locate the
camper, who finds more than he bargained
for in his rashly decided actions. For, as
he wanders in the fields, lost, alone and
scared, Ronnie unknowingly runs toward
the swelling river that will carry him to
an uncertain fate.

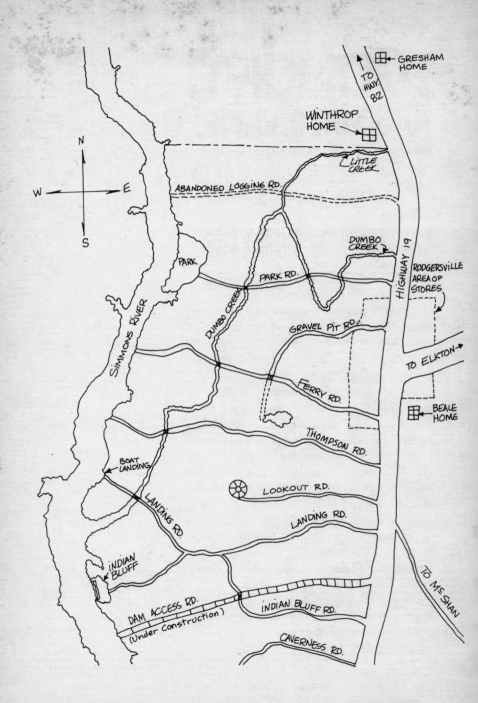

Weekly Reader Children's Book Club presents

EMERGENCY!
10-33 on channel 11!

by HILARY MILTON

Franklin Watts
New York / London / 1977

NOTE: Valid Citizens Band Radio call letters begin with the letter *K* (the author's call letters are KHM 8703). To avoid using the call letters of individuals now possessing valid licenses, the author has used *J* as the first letter in this book.

PACER: *P*olice *A*ssociated *C*itizens *E*mergency *R*adio Network. The members of this organization monitor channel 9, scheduled to provide around-the-clock coverage to aid motorists or others who need assistance.

REACT: *R*adio *E*mergency *A*ssociated *C*itizens *T*eams. REACT groups and organizations also monitor channel 9, and for the same reason.

Library of Congress Cataloging in
Publication Data

Milton, Hilary H
    Emergency! 10-33 on channel 11

    SUMMARY: A distress call sent over a
CB radio brings a rescue party to a camper
that has overturned on a lonely road.
    [1. Citizens band radio—Fiction. 2. Traffic
accidents—Fiction] I. Title.
PZ7.M6447Em   [Fic]   76-30292
ISBN 0-531-02905-0

This book is a presentation of
The Popcorn Bag
Weekly Reader Book Club

Weekly Reader Book Division offers book clubs for
children from preschool to young adulthood. All
quality hardcover books are selected by a distinguished
Weekly Reader Selection Board.

For further information write to:
Weekly Reader Book Division
1250 Fairwood Avenue
Columbus. Ohio 43216

Weekly Reader Children's Book Club Edition

Publisher's edition: $5.90

1/A

lec Horton opened the door and slid in under the steering wheel. As he shut the door, the light drizzle turned suddenly to hard rain. "Just made it."

Sitting beside him and watching the hard gusts cover the windshield with sliding sheets of water, Jane said, "Is mother all right?" Mrs. Horton was lying down in the camper and Jane's father had just gone back to look in on her.

"She's all right—a little tired, that's all. Maybe she shouldn't have eaten that egg salad sandwich for lunch."

They had been on the road since shortly after six o'clock that morning and, much as they all liked the camper, all of them were beginning to feel the effects of a full day's drive. Until last year, Jane thought, they usually flew to wherever they were going to spend the two-week vacation shortly after school was out. Mother, though, had gotten tired of flying—said she just didn't want to travel that way anymore. So when they got ready to make their journey last year—they'd gone to the eastern shore, then Chincoteague, Virginia, where the wild ponies were, and on down to Williamsburg—her father had bought the pickup truck and put the large camper body on it. Jane had halfway hoped he would get one of those big motor homes but he had decided against that. "They just sit in the driveway when you're not using them," he had said. "With the pickup, we can take the camper part off, use the truck like a car if we wish."

It hadn't made any difference, once they started using it. They had traveled comfortably, stopped when they wanted to, seen everything along the route and hadn't spent any time looking for motels. Jane had found it a lot more fun—they could go near the ocean or camp by lakes and rivers—even stopped one night on a mountaintop where there wasn't even a house or a motel in sight. Right now, however, she was a little tired, too—because it was the first day, she decided. She brushed both hands across her face and pushed loose strands of her shoulder-length hair back of her ears. "Are we going on?"

They were parked on a road shoulder and her father hesitated about starting up and pulling out. He took the small road map and angled it toward the door window. "Getting darker than usual for this time of day," he said. "Hard rain's coming—might be a good idea if we could find a roadside park."

"Is there one marked on the map?"

He waited a moment. "I don't see a sign," he said slowly. "But we're not too far from a river—looks like Simmons—"

"We crossed the Simmons River back a bit, just before we turned off the big highway onto this one."

"Well, it seems to flow south—couldn't be more than a mile or so west of this road." He put the map aside. "Tell you what, let's try the radio—maybe somebody can tell us if there's a park nearby."

The radio was a two-way Citizens Band unit her father had had installed last year after they got back from the vacation. On that journey he'd talked to lots of campers and he'd learned they all relied on them—kept up with where road detours were, listened out for "Smokey" reports, and got directions without having to stop at service stations. Mother had called it a toy, she'd sort of joked about it, saying the only difference between men and boys was the price of the toys they bought. But the radio had come in handy several times—so handy, in fact, that her father had bought a CB base station and had mounted a big antenna to the top of the chimney. He had learned the numbers called the 10-code—10-2, 10-4, 10-9, 10-27, 10-33, 10-36, and so on—and on nights when he didn't have to work or help her with her studies, he spent an hour or so talking to people he didn't know.

For a while, she had watched him and listened to the people "coming back," as they said—the names and call letters of CBers around the county. At first, she thought it was funny, hearing the names people gave themselves— Junkman, Dog-Catcher, Hogwash, Butterfly, Soupy, and so on—and she thought it even funnier when her father began calling himself Cornpone. The more she listened, however, the more fascinated she had become. And one day when he was at work, she'd gone on the air herself—given the call letters and talked to five different people. That night her mother had made her tell her father what she had done. She'd halfway expected him to tell her not to use it. Instead, he'd seemed pleased. "Well, she's eleven going on twelve," he had said. "About time to learn something new." He'd told her, though, to study the 10-code numbers if she wanted to use the radio. Now, she wasn't Jane Horton— she was JTZ 4061 and Popcorn.

It had taken a while to settle on the Popcorn handle. She had thought about calling herself Blue-Eyes or Blondie, or maybe Pretty One or Pixie Face—the various nicknames her father would give her from time to time. But they sounded too little-girlish or fancy—and she was getting bigger. She had finally settled on Popcorn because that seemed to go with Cornpone.

Alec turned on the switch and turned up the volume. Listening to the crackle of static, he took the microphone from its hook and held it to his mouth. But before pressing the "talk" key, he turned the channel selector from 19 to 11. "The truckers are on channel nineteen," he said. "Channel eleven is still the call channel for most people."

Jane nodded. "I remember—we used it last Christmas when we drove to Grandmother's."

Alec waited a moment, then pressed the button. ". . . Break-break."

A moment's quiet, then ". . . Go ahead, break-break on channel eleven."

Alec turned the volume higher. "Thanks for the break. . . . This is JTZ 4061 mobile. . . . I need a little assistance."

". . . Go ahead, JTZ 4061 mobile. . . . This is JLD 2221, the Logroller, I copy. . . . What do you need?"

". . . Do you know of a camper park nearby?"

A moment's pause, then, ". . . What's your ten-twenty, mobile?"

To herself, Jane translated 10-20 to "Where are you now?"

". . . About three miles south of Highway Eighty-two, State Highway Nineteen. . . ."

"Ten-four, ten-four—"

"He knows where we are," Jane said.

". . . Mobile, you're about three, three and a half miles north of a place called Rodgersville . . . little farm community. . . . They've got a park on the river near there . . . nothing fancy. . . . Do you have a big rig?"

"No, negative," Alec said. "Pickup with a camper body."

"Ten-four . . . won't have any trouble getting to it. . . ." the man calling himself Logroller said. "Keep on Route Nineteen for another five or six minutes, you'll come to a sign that says Rodgersville—that's R-o-d-g-e-r-s-v-i-l-l-e—another quarter of a mile and you'll see a two-story house to your right. . . . Got it?"

"I copy you, ten-four."

". . . Good. . . . Now, keep going past that house, take the second . . . repeat, second . . . gravel road to your right. . . . Takes you right to the park."

Alec glanced at Jane, then stared at the rain now beating hard on the windshield. ". . . Ten-four, Logroller . . . but with this rain . . . what about the gravel road?"

"No sweat, mobile . . . hard-packed all the way . . . nothing fancy about the park, though . . . water, picnic tables . . . think they put up some toilets last spring . . . it'll do for overnight parking. . . ."

"Ten-four, Logroller . . . thanks for the comeback. . . ."

"Any time, good buddy . . . JLD 2221, the Logroller down. . . ."

"Ten-four, JTZ 4061 clear." Alec put the mike back onto its clip. "Comes in handy," he said, nodding toward the radio.

Driving cautiously once he was back on the highway, Alec took almost fifteen minutes, though, getting to the Rodgersville Town Limits sign—so long that Jane was about to ask if maybe they'd passed it.

"There it is," she said when they came upon it. "Now—what did he say?"

"Look for a two-story house."

A moment later, she spotted the dwelling and pointed. "Not a lot of lights, but I guess that's it."

Alec had been driving with only his parking lights on, but as the rain got heavier, he switched to the main headlights. "The second road past it—that's what he said."

Less than a minute later, they came to a gravel and dirt turn-off. "Is that the first one?" Jane asked. "It sure doesn't look like much."

Alec stared at it. "No—just a field road. There," he said as they approached a wider one a quarter of a mile farther, "is the first one." Three hundred yards beyond, the headlights picked up another wide turnoff. "And this must be the second."

"Hope we didn't miss any."

"We didn't." When Alec turned onto it, he found that it was almost as firm as the blacktop. "Guess Logroller's right."

"I sure hope so," Jane said. "But, Daddy, isn't it a lot darker than it ought to be this time of the day—just a little before seven?"

"The clouds and the rain," Alec said.

He downshifted at a mudhole, then kept the pickup in second gear for what seemed like almost three-quarters of a mile. At the sharp left turn, he slowed down and maneuvered it, keeping the camper moving at a steady pace. "They need to fill in some chuckholes."

Jane bounced and slid forward, caught herself, and pushed back against the seat. "Sure am glad we don't have roads like this all the way to Florida."

They came to a place where the route they were following intersected another gravel road. The one they crossed seemed to be wider than the one they were on, and for a moment Alec hesitated, glancing in both directions. "Wonder if we took the right one."

"We did if we counted right."

Alec nodded and kept going straight. A hundred feet farther, however, his left front wheel dropped into a deeper ditch than the one they'd bounced over moments before. He braked hard, let the camper settle, then eased forward again, this time in the lowest gear. Another twenty feet and they were suddenly out of road altogether, with weeds coming right up to the top of the hood and the wheels following narrow, rutted paths. Close-growing tree limbs brushed the camper's side and all wheels seemed to keep hitting mudholes.

"Daddy! This doesn't look like any road at all!"

"It's not," he said tersely. "Should have turned at that other—" He broke off as he felt the left rear wheel slip to the side. Again, he braked hard and this time Jane slipped forward almost onto the floorboard.

"Daddy!"

"It's all right, honey." He tried to make his voice sound calm but Jane sensed a growing concern. "We'll just back out of here and take the other one—should have stopped at that house to make sure about the directions."

"I wish we had."

Alec eased the camper into reverse, tested the clutch, and gradually began moving backward. He rolled down the window and leaned partway out so he could see the back of the camper through the rearview mirror that was mounted on the side. Limbs scraped the side again. Rain made a sheet of water and covered the windshield. The headlights sent bobbling beams through the wet brush and woods.

Suddenly the left rear wheel caught at a mudhole, lurched hard, and dropped into a deep, washed-out ditch at the road's edge. The camper seemed to totter for a moment, then it tilted hard.

Just before it crashed violently on its left side, Alec Horton grabbed the ignition key and flipped it off. . . .

All the noise, all the limbs breaking, all the camper's violent shuddering—all of it suddenly died. Jane heard only the pounding rain, felt the driblets of it leaking through the right side window which had been left barely open to let in air. Somehow she had bumped her head—against the steering wheel, she guessed. It hurt some, but her left arm and shoulder hurt worse. Her legs were caught and twisted, her body pressed hard against her father; her left shoulder ached and somehow her arm had slipped and was caught between the seat and her father's back. "Daddy—can you move a little?"

He made no sound, no movement.

"Daddy!" She tried to look at his face but all she could make out was the vague silhouette. "Daddy! You're hurting my arm!"

Still no sound, no movement.

"Daddy! Daddy!"

This time, when he remained still and silent, the full impact of truth bore down on her. Unconscious, that's what he was, knocked out like he was dead asleep and she couldn't think of what you were supposed to do to make somebody quit being unconscious.

She tried to twist about but could not. She didn't like it, didn't like it at all, and she trembled. With her free right hand, she reached as far back as she could and knocked on the pickup's rear window. "Mama! Mama! Daddy's hurt and I can't move!"

The rain seemed to come harder so that all she heard was the closed-in sound of her own voice, caught inside the pickup's cab. And no answer from her mother.

Jane shuddered and trembled once more. She stared through the rain-fogged windshield toward the blurred glare of the headlights that pointed nowhere.

The headlights—wires and electricity and all that rain—Jane didn't know how such things were supposed to work, but somewhere she had read that if wires got wet they could short out and start a fire. She didn't know. Maybe it wasn't true—but maybe it was. Straining across as hard as she could, stretching her hand to the instrument panel, she found the headlight knob and pushed it in.

Instantly the cab was totally dark except for a slight glow from the CB radio's lighted meter and channel selector. The radio—it was right there in front of her, all she had to do was reach for the mike, call for the Logroller—maybe he was still on the air—tell him what had happened and to get help quickly, couldn't do anything by herself, all pinned down this way.

She made a grab for the mike and was just about to jerk it from its clip when she caught herself. Couldn't hurry, couldn't let it slip away. Let it fall and it could get twisted on something she couldn't see—maybe a broken pedal, maybe her father's leg or the gearshift lever.

Ever so cautiously she wrapped her fingers firmly about it before pulling it free. Though her hand was trembling, she made slow movements as she brought the mike to her mouth. She pressed the key. "Logroller . . . Logroller . . . do you still copy? This is JTZ 4061, Popcorn . . . Cornpone's daughter. . . . Logroller . . . we have an emergency. . . . WE HAVE AN EMERGENCY! A ten–thirty-three on channel eleven. . . ."

The speaker crackled when she let up on the key. Crackled and popped. Hummed and buzzed. But no voice came through it.

Again Jane pressed the key. "Logroller . . . JTZ 4061 . . . Logroller or somebody . . . anybody . . . emergency. . . . I have a ten–thirty-three on this channel. . . . Please . . . somebody answer. . . ."

2/Heavy raindrops made muted spats on the roof, a lulling sound that penetrated the even quietness inside the two-story Winthrop farmhouse. Thirteen-year-old David Winthrop and his eleven-year-old brother, Ronnie, were at their usual place on nights like this—at the long table in the dining/family room, each busy with his special project.

The day's mail had brought David the strobe-light kit he'd ordered three weeks earlier, and he was studiously going over the directions and detailed plans. Earlier, he had built a small transistorized radio, but somewhere he had read that it was possible to construct a color-varying light that would flicker to radio music tempo—*if* he could make the proper connections. Ronnie had already cut out the spars and struts for a model airplane and was now putting the pieces together.

"Shoot," David said suddenly.

"S'matter?" Ronnie asked without looking up.

"No terminals to make the radio hookup."

"I told you so."

"Told me what?"

"You should have ordered that from the same company you got the radio from."

"Don't see how that would matter—both catalogs gave the same information."

"Trouble with you is, you believe everything you read."

David put down the directions and watched his brother glue two strips of balsa to an oval-shaped fuselage part. "And the trouble with you is, you begin putting things together without reading at all."

"I get it right, though."

"Ha."

"Ha, yourself—I'll have this plane flying before you get that crazy light built."

"Bet a dime it'll never take off."

"Make it a dollar—"

"Boys, boys," Nell Winthrop said, coming through the door from the kitchen, carefully wiping her hands on the small print apron. "Just mind your business—both of you." She walked past them to the huge window and glanced out. "Looks like we're in for an all-night rain—lightning to the west."

"Wish it would stay west," Ronnie said. "Another gully washer like we had day before yesterday and the river'll cover the fields—"

"David," Nell interrupted, "where'd you leave the horses?"

"Oh, Lordy," and David pushed his chair back, "in the west pasture."

Ronnie dropped the piece he was gluing. "I thought you put 'em in the paddock this afternoon."

"I meant to," David said, "but Dad hollered for me to come help him unhook the discs. When it started raining and he had to hurry to get to that meeting, I just plain forgot." He dropped the direction sheet on the table. "We'd better go move 'em—if the river gets up, it'll flood the pasture."

"Maybe the rain'll stop soon." But Nell's voice had a note of uncertainty in it.

"Can't take a chance—Dad sure wouldn't like it if they got caught down there." David got up and turned to Ronnie. "Come on—won't take long to round them up and drive 'em uphill. Likely they're gathered at the oak banks anyway."

Ronnie screwed the top on the glue tube. "All except Old Shoe—she's liable to be anywhere."

"No sweat," David said. "Do like you always do—take an apple out there and bite into it a couple of times—she'll come to you like hogs heading for the swill."

As the boys walked through the kitchen and into the service room that separated the garage from the rest of the house, Nell watched their movements, more conscious than usual of how much they were growing, how different they were becoming, and yet how together they were when there was a need to be. David was growing taller—by the day, it seemed—and his shoulders were broad like his father's. His arms were long and sinewy, strong without being muscular. Except for the fact that his hair came down, tousled and loose, covering his collar, and black as pitch, he was the image of George Winthrop. Another four years and six or so inches, and they'd pass for twins—from the back, at least. Ronnie, she was reminded again, took after her side of the family. Shorter than David by half a head, with rust-red hair that was a bit more cared for than was his brother's, he had the overall stocky build of his grandfather Jesse—barrel-built, folks said. Already, he outweighed David by five pounds and wore the same size clothes—though she had to shorten his jeans. Different, she supposed as night and day, even to their dispositions. But the one common denominator was their sense of responsibility where the animals and chores were concerned. Right now, for example. Instead of blaming David for being thoughtless—as he might have done with books or games—Ronnie shared the immediate task as if he were equally responsible for leaving the horses.

"Both of you better take your flashlights," she called after them. She hesitated, then added, "Maybe you'd better take the walkie-talkies—it's pretty dark out there. *And* put on your raincoats."

"Aw, Mom," Ronnie hollered back, "do we *have* to? Raincoats get so hot and it won't take ten minutes."

"You have to," she said simply. That, she knew, was all she had to say. . . .

When the door shut after them and she knew they'd had time to get as far as the back gate, she turned off the kitchen light and stood at the window watching. A streak of lightning cut through the darkness and she wished that George hadn't gone to the District Farmers Association meeting down at Greensboro—meeting wouldn't end till after ten o'clock, he'd be after midnight getting home.

Nell was half-watching the beams from the boys' flashlights crisscrossing in the dark when the sharp ring of the phone broke the silence, startling her. She turned quickly about and felt for the wall receiver. "Hello."

The phone made a crackling sound, then nothing.

"Hello," she repeated.

Nothing.

For a moment longer she held the receiver, then slowly put it back on its hook. And that, she knew, was that. Somewhere in the maze of interconnecting wires, cables, and terminal boxes or whatever, something had broken down. The phones were out of order again—for how long this time, she could only guess. Two months earlier, the last week of April, they went out on Saturday afternoon and didn't come back until the following Thursday. This time it might be momentary—but she doubted it. Now—if George were late and had to call—well, he'd just better not be. . . .

"You got your walkie-talkie on?"

"Have to pull out the antenna first," Ronnie said.

"Okay—but be sure it's set on C-one."

"It stays on C-one, dummy."

"It's *supposed* to stay on C-one," David said, "but sometimes the switch gets bumped."

"Okay—but I checked," and he clicked the ON switch, pressed the transmit button.

David's walkie-talkie gave out a shrill squeal. "Hey! Cut it out—we're too close."

"Sorry," Ronnie said quickly. "I didn't mean to do that." He turned and started north, along the fence line. "I'll work this way to the old bored well—you go south to the fence line."

"Okay—but they'll most likely be where you said."

"Maybe—but they could be all the way to the plum thicket." Ronnie took half a dozen steps, then called over his shoulder. "First one that spots them, say so."

"Okay."

They moved apart slowly then, each sweeping the open field with his flashlight, and as they moved in separate directions each lost sight of the other. Fifty yards from the paddock gate, David spotted a quick movement and turned his light in that direction. A brown rabbit paused, hunched down, then suddenly bolted out of sight into a clump of briars. David looked after it for a moment, then continued his trek.

He was certain the horses would be near the oak banks, but when he got there and looked all around, he saw not even a hoofprint in the soft earth. He stopped and pressed the walkie-talkie's button. "Ronnie."

A pause, then, "Yeah?"

"They're not here."

"Are you at the oaks?"

"Right at 'em."

"Did you walk around 'em?"

"Around and through 'em, too. Nothing."

"Dumb horses." And brief static made Ronnie's voice crackle on David's walkie-talkie. "Okay—I'm at the old hickory stump now—heading toward the river path, going west."

"Ten-four," David said, mimicking the TV police and knowing Ronnie wouldn't like it.

"Ten-four, yourself—and cut it out, will you."

David grinned to himself and started moving toward the southwest fence intersection and the heavy foliage of the plum thicket. If they were there, he wouldn't be surprised, this time, to find Old Shoe with the others. He pressed the transmit button. "Ronnie?"

A pause, then, "Yeah?"

"See anything?"

"Not yet—and don't give me any of that ten-four stuff."

"Okay, okay," David said, "but turn your light on the sandpit when you go past it."

"I'm by it now—nothing."

"The plum thicket, then—they've got to be there."

"They'd better be—hey, this rain's really coming down."

David started to press the button to reply, but before he could do it, he heard a faint voice on the walkie-talkie. He stopped, waited. Nothing else. "Ronnie?"

"Did you find them?" Ronnie asked.

"No," David said slowly, "but did you hear something funny on your walkie-talkie just then?"

"Heard something. Maybe lightning. Or maybe it was that whatever-they-call-it—you know, what Mary Lou Gresham was yakking about at Sunday school." Mary Lou was Sam Gresham's daughter, same age as David and in the same grade. Her father had that big farm a quarter of a mile north on the other side of the highway. Mr. Gresham had one of those fancy Citizens Band radios with a tower and beams he could turn from inside the house.

"Skipper or skip or something like that."

"Yeah. Well, maybe that's what it was," Ronnie said. "Anyway, it wasn't horses and that's what we'd better find."

David flashed his light on a small trickly stream the rain had made, then leaped over it. "Where are you now?" he said into the mike.

"Just past the bored well—no sign of them."

"We'd just as well head straight for the plum trees."

"Sure hope they're there."

They were both moving toward the same northwest corner of the pasture, still more than a hundred yards away from each other when sheet lightning brightened the sky. Simultaneously, they heard the quick neighing. Ronnie keyed the walkie-talkie. "That's where they are, all right."

"Can you see them?"

"No, but I heard Silky."

"How," David asked, "do you know it was Silky?"

"Just do," Ronnie said. "She's got that funny sound like a whistle, you know, when she starts neighing." Silky was the gentlest of the five, a sorrel mare George Winthrop bought for his wife—went all the way to Memphis to get her.

"Okay," David said, "if you say so. But don't spook 'em —wait till I get there."

Two minutes later, both boys were at the side of the plum thicket away from the river, where the overhanging branches formed a windbreak shelter. All the animals except Old Shoe were clustered near the tallest trees. David stopped, then moved slowly toward them, talking easily. Ronnie stayed still on the opposite side, making certain they didn't wander off. "You got the halters?"

"Got 'em," David said.

"Loop Silky first—won't be hard with the others."

David paused, took a step, paused once more, then reached out and patted the mare's neck. "It's all right, girl, come on, now, easy, easy." Cautiously he slipped the loose rope loop over her head, held it, then gave the lead end to Ronnie. "Now Breezy," he said.

Within minutes they had all four. "Now, what about Old Shoe?"

"Dumb nag," Ronnie said. "Ought to let her get soaking wet."

David said, "Yeah," but he knew better. No matter what Ronnie might say, Old Shoe was his favorite. He fed her apples, slipped her sugar when nobody was looking, and wouldn't put the switch to her, no matter what she did.

She'd been their first—both had learned to ride on her, and none of the others was quite the pet she was. "Well, let's take these to the paddock, then we can look for her."

By the time they got there, however, the rain was falling harder and sheets of lightning were backlighting the clouds at more frequent intervals. "Maybe," Ronnie said, "we'd better go ahead and put 'em in the stalls."

"Right," David said. "Rain's going to come a gullywhopper."

Without pausing to shut the paddock gate, they led the four horses into the barn and to the stalls. They were just closing in the last one when they heard a fluttering neigh and a hoof strike a board. Simultaneously, they turned their flashlights to the barn's other side. There was Old Shoe, clearly observing them as if to say *what took you so long?* Ronnie laughed. "Wouldn't you know it—bet she's been there since we left the gate open." He crossed over to the older mare. "Okay, old girl—you outsmarted us. *Now* what?"

"Think we ought to put her in the other stall?" David asked.

"No use—she'd just work the boards loose like she always does. We'll just shut the barn doors—she'll be okay."

When they had the door secured, they started toward the house. Then, almost as if at a signal, they stopped and turned back to the paddock gate. That was one thing their father had taught them—no matter what else you do, keep the gates closed. Make it a habit, he'd often said.

They were just pulling it to when static on David's walkie-talkie cleared and they heard a faint ". . . *Anybody copy, please.* . . ."

Both boys stopped all motion. "That's a girl's voice," Ronnie whispered. "Wonder how far off—"

". . . *Please, does anybody copy.* . . ."

"No," David said softly, "too close and too clear."

"What does *copy* mean?"

"I think it means does anybody hear."

"But who around here has a walkie-talkie?"

"Maybe it's not a walkie-talkie—could be a real two-way radio—"

"... *Please, emergency ... does anybody copy.* ..."

3/ **"D**id you hear—did you hear what she said!"

"I heard," David whispered. "Maybe I can answer."

"Aw, she can't hear you—"

"We heard her. Maybe—" David pressed the walkie-talkie's transmit button. "I copy you. If you hear me, say 'I copy you, David.' "

"That's double dumb," Ronnie started to say, "and—"

Static crackled again, then, ". . . I . . . I copy you . . . David."

David felt a sudden prickly chill at the back of his neck and along his arms. He looked quickly at Ronnie. "You hear—you hear that?"

"Yeah, yeah—wonder who she is and where she's talking from and what it's all about—"

". . . David, I copy you. . . . If you still copy, come back . . . please . . . emergency!"

"Emergency?" Ronnie said. "What's it? What does she mean?"

David's hand was beginning to tremble. He keyed the walkie-talkie once more. "I still copy you. What do you mean, emergency?" He paused, then added into the mike, "What's your name?"

". . . This is JTZ 4061 mobile . . . name is Jane Horton . . . camper's turned over—" But before she could complete what she was saying, lightning flashed to the west and crackling static drowned out the rest of her transmission.

David keyed the walkie-talkie. "Jane Horton . . . Jane Horton. . . . I didn't hear all of that."

In the moment's silence that followed, with only static coming from the walkie-talkie speaker, David had the sinking feeling that he could not hear her any longer, that the slim contact was broken and that whatever her emergency was—

"David . . . David, do you still copy?" The voice was fainter, and David couldn't be certain whether he could answer.

"Jane . . . Jane, I still copy . . . heard you say camper turned over. But where?"

"I . . . I don't know . . . a dirt road going toward a river . . . a road sign said Rodgersville. . . ."

Ronnie grabbed David's arm. "Did you hear that?" Rodgersville was the name of the small community they lived in. Their farm was about one mile north of the town's crossroads—a town made up of three general merchandise stores, a small post office, two filling stations, three churches, and a small white concrete block building called the Town Hall. Home to those who lived in Rodgersville, a wide place in the road on State Highway 19 to those passing through.

"I heard," David said.

"Ask her which road she's on?"

David pressed the transmit button once more. "Do you know which road you're on?"

A brief hesitation, then, "No . . . we're from Missouri . . . looking for a place to camp . . . but we need help . . . need help badly." Static garbled the transmission, then she came back. "Camper's on its side, my father's un—" She paused. "Unconscious . . . pinned under the steering wheel. . . .

My mother is in the camper"—her voice broke—"and I can't hear her. . . ."

Ronnie hastily pulled the latch on the paddock gate, whirled about toward his brother. "What'll we do?"

David swung the flashlight in a southward arc, as if somehow he could pick out a camper turned over down that way. "I—I don't know."

"We've got to do something—wish Dad was here."

David wished so, too, but he wasn't—and neither were any of the other farmers in the town. Like his father, they'd all gone to the Association meeting, no telling when they'd get back.

He couldn't wait, yet he was faced with something he'd never before experienced. "Tell you what—wait, try your walkie-talkie, see if you can talk to her."

"What'll I say?"

"Anything—say you're my brother, see if she can copy you—"

"All this *copy* business and ten-fours, I don't know how to use it like a real radio—"

"You *have* to."

"Aw, David—I just don't know about all this—"

"Just press the button, like you do when we talk—ask her if she hears you, tell her your name."

"Then what?"

"Then tell her"—David thought it and spoke it at the same time—"tell her I'm going to look for help. You'll stay here and keep contact—"

"Keep contact? What's that supposed to mean? And where are you going?" Ronnie's voice was uncertain, reflecting, David thought, the old staying-in-the-dark fears.

"Talk—so she'll know somebody's still listening to her.

I'm going to the phone. I'll talk back to you while M
calls—don't worry."

"Well"—Ronnie took a deep breath—"if I have to—but
I'm staying right here by the gate—don't you forget that."

"I won't. Now—press the button and talk."

Ronnie hesitated, held the walkie-talkie close to his face,
slowly pressed the "talk" button. "Jane, this is Ronnie—
I'm David's brother—do you hear me?"

Lightning flashed again, the static crackled louder. Then,
". . . I copy you . . . Ronnie. . . . Please help us . . . *please*."

Ronnie turned to David. "Now what'll I say?"

"Tell her I'm going for help—but you'll stay right here so
she'll know somebody's in contact."

"Aw"—and David recognized Ronnie's wavering willing-
ness to stay outside alone—"we can't do anything."

"Suppose," David said firmly, "we were where she is—in a
strange state. We'd sure like somebody to help us."

"Well—okay," Ronnie said slowly. "But hurry, will
you?"

David ran across the paddock lot, jumped up the three
steps and almost skidded on the rear-porch floor. "Mom!
Mom! Troubles! We've got to call the sheriff!"

Nell flicked on the light and hurried to the door. "What?"

"People in trouble," David said. "You have to call the
sheriff—they've got to get here quick, people are trapped—"

"Now, wait a minute, not so fast," Nell said. "Slow down
and tell me what you mean."

Hastily, David told her about the calls on the walkie-
talkie, about the girl and the camper, about promising to
get help.

"The horses," Nell interrupted.

"In the barn," David said. "But you've got to call
sheriff—"

Nell shook her head. "The phone's dead."

"Oh, no—not again!" David felt the pain and tension building inside. "But they're out there, maybe hurt!"

Nell glanced at the electric clock that told them it was fifteen minutes till nine. "Are you real sure about it, son?"

"We heard her—both of us did. Here"—he started toward the door to the back porch—"come on and listen for yourself."

Nell hesitated, then said, "Maybe I'd better."

They moved to the edge of the porch and David aimed the walkie-walkie's antenna as straight up as he could without touching the roof's overhang. He pressed the "talk" button. "Ronnie?"

A moment's pause, then, "Yeah?"

"Did she say anything else?"

"Just keeps saying hurry—says she thinks her father's arm is pinned but she's not sure."

David looked at his mother. "See?"

"You try to talk to her," Nell said.

Once more David keyed the walkie-talkie. "Jane . . . Jane Horton, this is David . . . do you copy?"

Static crackled when he unkeyed, then the faint voice came: ". . . David . . . I copy"—her voice was weak and the signal was faint—"can you get help for us . . . hurry. . . ."

David looked at his mother. "See?"

Nell nodded quickly. "We'll do something. But ask her if she can give you any idea what road she's on, anything."

Once again, David pressed the button. "Jane Horton . . . David again. . . . What road are you on? . . . Do you remember anything about it?"

". . . We saw a Public Park sign on the highway . . . didn't have an arrow . . . but the rain . . . don't know which side road we took. . . ."

"Do you remember anything . . . *anything* . . . special."

". . . Static. . . . David . . . please repeat."

"Do you recall anything special about the road you took?"

"No. . . . Wide at first, got narrow . . . weeds and trees close to it . . . bouncy mudholes and a ditch. . . ." Her voice began to break, as if she were starting to cry but trying to hold back. "I can't move. . . ."

"Jane . . . Jane . . . try to take it easy—" He glanced at his mother for confirmation. "We'll get help."

"Please . . . and hurry."

David turned to his mother. "Now, do you believe—"

"I never doubted you," she broke in. "But I needed to be sure where she is." She stared off into the night. "One thing's sure—she's not on the park road." Once more lightning backlighted the clouds. "They could be on any one of those eight or nine farm roads."

"But which?" David turned the walkie-talkie off, then on again. "We can't just wait, though—got to do something, start searching—"

"Well," said Nell firmly, "you and Ronnie can't do it—and all the men are down at Greensboro."

"How about Mr. Crockett? And Ray and Junior Gunnels?"

"Mr. Crockett's too old—you know that." Nell stopped as distant thunder rumbled once more. "And Ray and Junior went to Texas for that rodeo."

"Then what about T. C. Parsons?"

"T. C. took a job over in Jasper—comes home only on weekends."

"Well," David said impatiently, "there has to be somebody with cars—we can go find a few."

"Your father took the car and you know I can't drive the truck."

"I can take the garden tractor—"

"No," Nell said firmly, "your father wouldn't have you take it on the road at night."

David walked around the kitchen, returned to the window, and stared out. "But we have to do something—we can't just stand here. No telling about those people."

"If there was just some way"—and Nell glanced at the useless telephone—"to get in touch with the sheriff's office."

David stared out at the night a moment longer, looking at the lightning-fringed clouds. Then he snapped his fingers and whirled about. "The Greshams! I can go down there—"

"What for?"

"That two-way radio—Citizens Band—you know, like the walkie-talkies except bigger and stronger. Maybe Mary Lou can call the sheriff with it."

"Can she operate it?"

"She's always spouting off about talking to people in Columbus and Grayson—said one night she talked to a man in Memphis."

Nell sighed heavily. "I just don't know—"

"David?" It was Ronnie on the walkie-talkie.

"Yeah?"

"Did you call the sheriff?"

"Phone's out of order," David said flatly.

"Well, how much longer have I got to stay out here?"

David turned to his mother, handed her the walkie-talkie. "You tell him—I'm going to the Greshams. Maybe she can operate the thing herself." He turned and started toward the front door. "I'll take the flashlight. And don't worry—

I'll stay out of the road. And if I'm not right back you'll know I'm trying to help—"

At that moment, the lights in the house flickered, went off, came on once more, then went out. "Oh, no," Nell said. "Not that, too."

"Mom"—it was Ronnie on the walkie-talkie—"what's happened?"

Nell pressed the key. "The lights are out—but don't worry, just stay where you are and keep your flashlight on." She lowered the walkie-talkie. "There's no point in going now, no electricity."

"Some radios work on batteries," David said. "Maybe Mr. Gresham's does—anyway, won't take long to find out."

"Well, all right—but before you go, let me use the flashlight long enough to find some candles."

Outside once more, with his flashlight jiggling as he half-trotted, half-walked the quarter of a mile up the road toward the Gresham house, David tried to count the possible dirt and gravel roads that turned toward the river from the state highway—the old ferry road, the lookout road, the old landing road—and all the others—

The thought hurried him along. If the river rose, they'd all be flooded in no time. No doubt about it, those people needed lots of help—more than he and Ronnie and maybe two or three others could give them. Just had to get in touch with the sheriff's office. One thing he was glad of— Sheriff Tate knew his family and would know him well enough to believe him. And the Greshams.

If they could get in touch with Sheriff Tate.

And that depended on Mary Lou—or her mother.

He almost stopped. Mrs. Gresham—he'd completely forgotten about her. She'd be nice, but she just might say nobody was going to use that Citizens Band radio without Mr. Gresham being there.

But he had to try, anyway. He flashed the light ahead and hurried on, this time trotting all the way.

At his knock on the huge double door, he heard footsteps and the motion of a hand on the knob. When it opened a crack, he caught the yellow glow of four candles on the mantle. "Yes?"

He could just make out Mrs. Gresham's face in the semi-dark. "Me—David Winthrop—and Mrs. Gresham," he almost blurted, "we need help."

She opened the door wider, and he saw she was wearing one of those western skirts, looked like leather almost. "Your mother's sick—"

"Oh, no, ma'am"—noting that Mary Lou had joined her mother, David seemed to stumble on his words—"it's some other people, Hortons—"

"Hortons?" Mrs. Gresham repeated. "I don't know any Hortons."

"They're not from here," David said quickly. Then, looking down to make sure he didn't have mud on his shoes, he told them how he and Ronnie came to know about the turned-over camper.

"Should have known better," Mrs. Gresham said. "But, David, our phone's out of order, too."

"I know," Mary Lou added, "I just tried to call Sara Pinson."

"Well"—and now that he was at the subject, David wasn't sure he'd made the right decision—"you do have that two-way radio."

"The CB?"

He nodded. "I thought—you know, just maybe you could use it, maybe the sheriff or somebody would hear you."

"The sheriff's people don't use CB—they have their own radios."

"I was afraid of that but I couldn't think of anything else."

"But maybe," Mary Lou picked up, "we could call somebody else—a mobile—and they'd get the message to the sheriff."

David looked up quickly. "If you could do that—"

"Oh, no." And Mary Lou made a face. "Lights are out—no power."

"What a time for *that* to happen," Mrs. Gresham said. She came out onto the porch and looked up the highway, toward Rodgersville, as if hoping to see somewhere up the way a sign that lights were coming back on. "Her father doesn't like for her to use the radio when he's not here, but we could—except we can't."

David felt shaky all over. "Then I don't know what to do. Mom can't drive the truck, the tractor doesn't have lights, just no way"—he caught himself, added quickly—"it won't work on batteries?"

Mary Lou seemed to think for a minute. "Wait, that's right—it's a base/mobile radio, could be used in a car. But we don't have a battery inside."

"Maybe there's one at my house."

Mrs. Gresham caught his arm. "Wait—Sam put a new one in the pickup yesterday, said the old one had about had it. But it may have enough life in it to run the radio." She paused, then added, "Trouble is, I don't know how to hook it up."

David looked at Mary Lou. "Do you?"

"I know which wire's positive and which is negative—but I don't know where they go on the battery."

"I know the positive and negative battery terminals," David said.

"Well"—Mrs. Gresham made a quick move toward the door—"it's in the shed back of the garage. The light switch—" She caught herself.

"I've got the flashlight."

"You'll have to look for it."

David started around the porch that made an "L" beside the house and acted as a breezeway to the garage. "I'll find it," he said.

As she stepped inside the front room, Mrs. Gresham paused. "When you get it, come to the back door—the radio's in the room off the kitchen."

The shed was unlocked, nothing but a slip latch holding the door closed. David opened it and went inside, immediately aware of the dank smell of oil and engines and cleaning equipment. As he flashed the light about, he saw that the shed's walls were covered with pegboards, all spaces carefully labeled for tools—wrenches, hammers, files, saws, and saw blades, and at the rear of the room was a workbench built of heavy timber with a vice at one end and the motorized part of a lathe at the other. He flashed the light about the floor and under the workbench until it came to rest on the old battery. Mr. Gresham had left the lift handle on it, still attached to the terminals. Before he started to reach for it, he picked up an electrical wire-peeler and a pair of pliers and shoved them in his pocket.

The battery was heavier than he'd expected and coated with greasy grime. Ought to clean it off, he thought—but no time for that.

When he got to the back door, he rapped hard, then

waited for Mary Lou to open it. "Better put some news-papers on the floor," he said. "Battery's pretty dirty."

It took them five minutes to get the battery in place, wipe the terminals clean, and spot the plus and minus posts. Taking the wires Mary Lou handed him and hurrying as fast as he could in the dim candlelight, he cleared the insula-tion, scraped the bare copper wires, and wrapped them onto the terminal posts.

"You're sure you didn't reverse them?" Mary Lou asked. "If they're backward, they'll burn out the radio."

David looked quickly at the red wire going to the positive terminal, the black one going to the negative. "I'm sure."

"Well, here goes." She reached behind the radio and turned the antenna connection until she could no longer twist it. "That better be in place—oh, gosh, I forgot!"

"Now what?" Mrs. Gresham asked.

"The beams—they have to be rotated by house current."

"Will they work anyway?" By her question, David guessed that Mrs. Gresham never fooled with the CB.

"They'll work," Mary Lou said, "but the signal won't be the best if they're not pointed right—"

"Try, anyway," her mother said. "Maybe somebody'll hear."

Mary Lou checked the DC cord plug-in once more, then turned the ON switch. Nothing happened. "Oh, no!"

"What?"

"No power still!"

4/David looked down at the wires going to the battery. "But I *know* those are the right terminals. See?" And he turned the flashlight on the *plus* and *minus* marks. "Is it still plugged to the wall?"

"I'd already pulled it out—we always do when the weather gets bad," Mary Lou said.

"Well"—David wracked his brain for a thought—"does it have a switch when you go from house current to battery?"

Mary Lou shook her head.

David stared at the radio, at the wires leading from it, and at the battery itself, as if something he'd missed would be evident. Finally he sighed heavily. "Maybe the battery's just plain dead." He thought a moment longer, then reached for the pliers. "There's one sure way to find out."

"What are you about to do?" Mrs. Gresham asked.

David opened the pliers, carefully bent down and put one grip end on one terminal, then slowly moved the tool toward the other. "If it sparks," he said, "we'll know."

"You're liable to get shocked—"

The second grip end contacted the opposite terminal and sharp, blue-yellow sparks flashed against the floor.

"David!"

"It's good," he said. "It's the contacts." He turned to Mrs. Gresham. "If I had something to clean those things—"

"A rag? I've got plenty—"

"Steel wool," David said quickly.

Without a word, Mrs. Gresham took a candle and hurried into the kitchen. While she was gone, Mary Lou turned to him. "Do you know what you're doing?"

David almost said *sure, I do* but right now was no time to be carelessly hasty. "Not about radios—but I've watched Dad, and I know dirty terminals may keep cars and tractors from starting."

"Well, I hope that's all we need," Mary Lou said. "My father will be mad as hops if we do anything to this CB."

Mrs. Gresham returned with a scrub pad and handed it to David. Wordlessly, he squatted down and rubbed around and over both battery posts. Grime greased his fingertips and knuckles but that didn't matter—main thing was to make good contact. When he was certain he'd gotten all the loose coating off, he once more wrapped the red wire to the positive terminal, the black one to the negative. He twisted them, then crimped them even more firmly with the pliers. He leaned back on his heels. "Do you have any electrical tape?"

"Should be some in the shed."

He got up quickly and started for the door, then remembered what a job it would be, finding black tape in the dark room. "Wait—do you have any rubber bands?"

"I've some in the kitchen drawer," Mrs. Gresham said.

"What are you going to do with rubber bands?" Mary Lou asked. "Won't they get hot and melt?"

"Terminals don't get hot," he said.

Mrs. Gresham returned in a moment with a fistful of all sizes. Selecting two wide, thick ones, David squatted down and wrapped them around the posts, binding the radio wires as tightly as he could. "Now," he said slowly, "if that doesn't work, I don't know what to do."

"Do you want me to try it now?"

He looked at the connections once more. "Might as well."

"Then here goes." Mary Lou sat at the chair her father used, held a candle so it lighted the several knobs, then deliberately clicked the ON switch.

Instantly, the signal meter light glowed yellow, a red needle within it began wavering, and a dial on the right-hand side of the radio turned white and glowed behind a numbered setting. The number was 15.

"You did it!" Mary Lou said.

David commenced wiping the grime onto his jeans. "Now —do you think you can call somebody?"

"I can try." Mary Lou turned the big numbered dial from 15 to 22, clicked it once more, and the static died.

"Something wrong?"

"No," she said quickly, "that's the public address spot —but never mind," and she turned it again. This time the number 23 showed up; static crackled from the speaker. "Before I try to raise somebody else, maybe we'd better go back to that girl—what's her name?"

"Jane," David said. "Jane Horton."

"What channel?"

"Hunh?"

"What channel was she on?"

"I don't know what you mean."

"What channel did you talk to her on?"

"I don't know anything about channels—we just have walkie-talkies."

Mary Lou pointed to the big knob she'd been turning. "You saw those numbers on the dial—each one's a separate channel. Which one's on your walkie-talkie?"

David concentrated. Come to think of it, there were

several numbers on the back of it—model number, FCC something-or-other—and he remembered the letters *Mhz,* but for the life of him, he couldn't remember anything about channels. "I just plain don't know."

"All right—is the walkie-talkie a good one?"

"I think so. Dad paid almost sixty dollars including tax for mine and Ronnie's."

"They're good ones," Mary Lou said flatly. "That means they probably have channel eleven in them." And without explaining how she knew that, she began turning the lighted numbers-dial once more. David watched as she passed 9, 10, then stopped at 11. The radio had a buzzing hum to it, and once in a while, as he watched the meter needle, it jumped up, then settled back to a measurement he couldn't make out. "Now," Mary Lou said, "did she use call letters?"

"She used some numbers but I don't remember them."

"Usually," she said, picking up the mike from its hook, "you don't use real names—call letters and handles are what people use, but I'll go with just Jane Horton." She held the microphone close to her mouth at an angle. "Break-break," she said in a clear, very firm voice, "JBK 9119 calling Jane . . . Jane Horton. If you copy me, Jane, come back."

Wordlessly, David watched as she moved the mike, concentrated on the radio, and seemed to be keeping her eye on the meter. *Come back,* he supposed, meant for Jane to reply.

But Jane did not reply, did not break the hum and crackling sounds coming from the speaker. Mary Lou waited several seconds, then she adjusted another knob. Once more she held the mike to her mouth and pressed the key. "Break-break . . . JBK 9119 calling Jane Horton . . . JBK 9119 calling Jane Horton. . . . If you copy, Jane, come back to this. . . ." She glanced quickly at David. "Bluebird."

Bluebird?

"That," Mary Lou said to him, as if she were reading his thought, "is the handle I use."

"Okay," he said, "if you say—"

"Break-break . . . JTZ 4061 mobile . . . I copy you, Bluebird. . . . This is a ten–thirty-three. . . ."

"Ten-four," Mary Lou said. "Did you talk to David and Ronnie?"

"Ten-four." Jane's voice seemed fainter than David remembered. "We need help . . . badly. . . . Do you copy?"

"I copy you," Mary Lou said. "Stand by . . . we are trying to get help. . . . But do you know what your ten-twenty is?" Once more she looked at David. "Ten–thirty-three means 'emergency' and ten-twenty means 'where are you?' "

David scratched his head. "It's a lot simpler to use the walkie-talkie—"

"I—I don't know," Jane said. "A dirt road . . . weeds and mud everywhere . . . slippery. . . ." Her transmission ended abruptly.

"JTZ 4061 mobile," Mary Lou said quickly, "do you still copy?"

A long pause, then, "Ten-four. . . . But my father just made a groaning sound. . . . He's hurt."

"Any other injuries?"

"I don't know."

David leaned closer. "She said her mother is in the camper —must be the back part."

Mary Lou nodded, held the mike closer to her mouth.

"JTZ 4061 mobile, this is Bluebird. . . . Stand by on channel eleven . . . I'm going ten–twenty-seven to other channels to get help. . . . And *we will get help."*

There was another code number, 10-27, David thought. But this time he figured it out. Mary Lou was going to change from channel 11 to the others—all the others, he supposed—in an effort to contact the sheriff.

She turned the big dial and David heard four clicks. The number 15 showed on the dial. "Break-break," Mary Lou said. "We have a ten–thirty-three . . . repeat . . . a ten–thirty-three . . . does anybody copy?" She let off the mike button and glanced at David. "Channel fifteen's the home channel around here—don't know who might be on the air."

David listened intently as the speaker hummed. But no answering voice broke through.

Again, Mary Lou adjusted the knob on the radio. "Break-break . . . repeat, we have a ten–thirty-three . . . emergency . . . on this channel. . . . Anybody copy?"

The same hum and static crackle followed.

"Power," Mary Lou said. "Power's out everywhere. Either that or everybody's disconnected because of the storm."

For the first time since he had first heard Jane on the walkie-talkie, David sensed the full impact of their isolation. He shook his head. "But what're we going to do? We can't just leave those people—"

"The radio has twenty-three channels," Mary Lou broke in. "We'll just have to try them all."

For the next five minutes, David watched helplessly as she turned the dial one click at a time, paused, pressed the mike button and repeated the "10-33" message. At the number "9" on the dial, she glanced at him. "That's the emergency channel, especially if you're on the highway. Lots of places even have organizations like PACER and REACT that monitor nine day and night." She keyed the mike and repeated the message on channel 9, waited, made the call again.

No response.

"Trouble is," she said, "most people around here don't use it much." She turned to 19 and, without glancing at him, said, "Nineteen's the one truckers use to talk to one another."

Again, however, her call received no response. She moved to 20, 21, and 22—and got nothing. "Nobody—nobody. Base stations are all out and no mobiles around."

David suddenly felt weak and worn and defeated. He'd been so sure she could help. "If Mom could just drive the truck—"

"Or if I could drive at night," Mrs. Gresham said. "But eyedrops I have to use keep my eyes from dilating—" She interrupted herself. "Helpless—that's what we are. And that poor little girl, she must be frantic. . . ."

5/Ronnie walked around the huge oak tree, counting the number of steps it took. He flashed the light at the paddock fence; then he walked to the watering trough and wished for the dozenth time that David would come on back—he didn't like being out here in the dark by himself.

He flicked on the walkie-talkie switch and heard nothing but static. He pressed the "talk" button. "Mom . . . are you still listening?"

"I'm listening, Ronnie."

"Where's David and why doesn't he come on back out here?"

"He went to the Gresham's—ought to be home soon."

"Well, I wish he would hurry."

He released the button. Dumb, just plain dumb, that's what it was. Anybody with good sense ought to know not to go toward the river on a night like this—camping park wasn't all that great, just a big open space, nobody used it except when they wanted to have a watermelon cutting; people that didn't know the country ought to stay out of side roads.

He stared off toward the river, halfway listening to the static and noise from the walkie-talkie, half-watching the outline of clouds the sheet lightning made. He was glad it wasn't his family off in a camper, turned over somewhere; even if they might have a radio in the car, he wouldn't know how to use it; that little girl, about his age, he supposed, felt real sorry for her out there, couldn't talk to her mother, didn't know how badly hurt her father was. It wouldn't be so bad, he guessed, to say something to her, let her know somebody was still around.

He raised the walkie-talkie to his mouth, thought about what he could say. He touched the "talk" button, hesitated, then pressed it. "Jane . . . Jane Horton, this is Ronnie. . . . Do you"—he still didn't feel comfortable using those words —"copy me?"

He let off the button and listened to the static. "Ronnie . . . mobile JTZ 4061 . . . this is Jane Horton. . . . I copy you. . . . Is anybody coming now?"

"I don't know," he answered. "David's trying to find help." As he talked, he slowly turned, pointing the antenna upward at a 45-degree angle and sweeping it in an arc.

"Ten-four . . . Bluebird called from her base . . . but tell them to please hurry . . . sounds like water's making puddles. . . ."

Bluebird? Didn't make any sense. He hadn't heard anything. Of course, he did turn the walkie-talkie off for a while. But Bluebird? He shook his head. Poor Jane Horton, must be hurt bad, out there in the dark hearing things. But the water, now, that wasn't hearing strange things. He knew the river was already rising and they might be too close. Or maybe the flatland where they were was flooding. He turned the flashlight west, as if he could spot the water on the lower fields. Funny thing, he thought, when he turned the antenna while she talked, she sounded faint, then stronger, then fainter again. Gave him an idea. He pressed the "talk" button once more. "Jane . . . I wonder . . . can I try something?"

A pause, then, "What?"

"I just may know which direction you're in. . . ." He didn't, but if the sound was stronger when he pointed the antenna in a certain direction, they might be turned over that way. "If you can talk . . . you know . . . if you can—he thought of the right word—transmit extra long, I'll turn the walkie-talkie . . . maybe find out something."

"Ten-four . . . but please, please tell them to hurry. . . . I'm scared and the rain's coming in . . . can't close the window . . . horn won't work . . . and I'm afraid to turn on the lights, might start a fire."

As she talked, Ronnie swept the antenna in an arc once more, right, then back to the left. He'd imagined it before, but now he was sure. Her voice got loudest when he pointed it southwest, toward where Dumbo Creek emptied into the river. Couldn't be on the Park Road. He thought hard. Might just be on that abandoned logging road that cut through the old Moreland place.

"Mom!" he said into the walkie-talkie. "Mom—I know where that camper's turned over."

A moment's silence, then, "Ronnie, how do you know?"

"I pointed the antenna—I just know." He thought a moment. "Has David gotten home?"

"He'll be home soon."

Ronnie didn't like that, darkness all around, but he suddenly made up his mind—and never mind the dark. "Tell him I'm walking across the Moreland place—they're on that old logging road—"

"You'd better wait—don't go wandering off by yourself."

"But they're really in trouble," he said, "and anyway, I know all about that field, can't get lost—I'll talk back to you." If he had not been so sure, Ronnie would be feeling his own uncertainty about being out in the dark alone. When he was little, he'd always liked a light on in his room, hadn't liked the dark at all, he'd heard his mother and father say something about his being afraid of the dark, never did let on he'd heard but it wasn't fear, he wasn't afraid, just didn't like it, that's all. And that was when he was little. Right after his tenth birthday, he'd turned that light off one night, hadn't bothered him, wasn't ever going to bother him again. Still, right now if he didn't *know* he'd find them on that old road and just *know* he'd be the first one to reach them, he supposed he would wait for David—two could look better than one.

"Ronnie, I don't think you should—mighty dark in the field."

He knew Mom was thinking about how it used to be, started to say the dark wouldn't bother him but he didn't want her to know that he knew what she was thinking. Anyway, he knew just exactly where he was going. Wouldn't take long to get there. "Won't take long," he said. "Just tell David and them that I know where the camper is. . . ."

David felt hurt and sore and angry at everything and everybody as he trotted home from the Greshams'. It *had* to happen this one night, men all down at that Association meeting, rain still falling, coming harder, lights out and anybody else that had a CB base station off the air, no telephones—if Dad would just hurry on home, he'd know what to do. One of the men could go get the sheriff, they could start searching. Time was going by, he guessed an hour had already passed since he and Ronnie first heard Jane, no telling how much longer they'd been there.

If he could just drive the tractor or the truck— he

stopped. But wait, maybe he couldn't drive but he could take Old Shoe, one thing about Old Shoe, she was as sure-footed as a goat, he could ride her uptown, maybe find some of the people who hadn't gone to the meeting. And Donna Beale, he could sure find her. She was grown, had her own truck, handled that herd of cows like she was a man. Never in his life did he remember seeing her wear a dress, always had on working jeans and a plaid shirt with the sleeves rolled up; she was older, twenty-three or twenty-four, he thought—but she'd help.

At home once more, he hurried around and went in the back door. The little candle flames flickered when he entered. "No luck," he said before his mother had a chance to ask a question.

She was seated at a chair near the window, looking out at the night that was now more frequently lit by sheet lightning. She glanced at him quickly. "With the power out, I guess you couldn't get the radio to work."

"Oh, we got it working all right—used an old truck battery. But nobody else was on." He stopped at the door leading into the kitchen and looked down at the water dripping from his raincoat. He wiped the flashlight on a cup towel by the counter. "Rain's coming a little harder—" He caught himself. "Ronnie—is he still out in the paddock?"

"I don't know what he's up to," she said. "Told me on the walkie-talkie he knew where the camper was—"

"How'd he find out?"

"I don't know," she said. "But he struck out walking across the Moreland place."

"That's lowland," David said quickly. "Likely water's already creeping over it."

"Oh, good Lord." And she got up, moved closer to the window. She held the walkie-talkie close to the screen and keyed it. "Ronnie—Ronnie, do you hear me? You'd better come back."

They both listened. No reply.

Once more she pressed the button. "Ronnie! I think you'd better come back—David's home now."

Again they listened. Once more, no reply.

She turned to David. "Something's happened—"

"No, Mom," he interrupted. "If he's set out walking, he probably turned it off and collapsed the antenna—you know, it's hard to walk in the dark with those long things."

"I hope you're right."

"Don't worry—if I know Ronnie, he'll walk a hundred yards then give it up and come back."

"Maybe," she said, but she did not sound convinced.

"Anyway," David added, "he knows every furrow on the place." He half-turned toward the back door.

"Where are you going?"

"Thought I'd saddle Old Shoe and ride up to Donna Beale's—she's got that truck, maybe she can look along some of the roads."

"Donna knows them," Nell admitted, "but with Ronnie out there—"

"He'll come back," David insisted. "But those poor people in that camper need help badly."

Nell seemed to hesitate. "Well—maybe it'd be a good idea. But hurry—you may have to look for Ronnie, too."

Ten minutes later, David guided Old Shoe up the driveway and onto the path that ran along the highway. She moved as surely as if it were broad open daylight, along a route she'd followed many times. Though he was in a hurry, David knew better than to urge her forward—the shoulder of the road was not wide and he didn't want her on the blacktop any more than necessary.

The mile ride, though, didn't take as long as he might have expected. They rode past the darkened stores, past the parking space on the other side of the Baptist church, past the little town hall and old Mr. Johnson's filling station, past the turnoff to the cemetery. A hundred yards beyond it, he carefully guided Old Shoe across the road toward an outlined driveway and the white picket fence surrounding the Beale's wide yard. At the gate, he stopped and flashed the light.

"Who's there?"

Donna Beale's voice was loud and clear. "Me, David Winthrop—is that you, Donna?"

"It is—what kind of trouble brings you out, a night like this?"

David slipped from the saddle and tied the reins to the gate post. That's how it was in Rodgersville—anything out of the ordinary and everybody knew trouble was in the wind. He opened the gate, keeping his light on the walkway, and hurried to the porch.

Donna was standing at the top of the steps when he reached the house. Nobody would ever mistake her for being what you'd call pretty—heavy legs, squared-off body, big shoulders and muscles more like a man than a woman. Kept her hair long, but David couldn't remember ever seeing her without one of those wide-billed caps perched on the back of her head. He kept the flashlight beam from shining right on her, but even in the side glow he could tell she was wearing one now. "Real trouble," he said, and told her what it was.

"Crazy city slickers," she said. "People who don't know any better than that ought to keep to the main roads and big motels." She half-turned toward the side of the porch where the wide swing was, and David could barely make out the form of Mrs. Beale. "Mama, you heard him—guess I'd better join the hunt."

"Take care, you hear." Mrs. Beale's voice was a low monotone. Folks said it never changed pitch, not since Mr. Beale died.

Donna glanced at David. "Better take Little Joe." She had a big truck but David knew "Little Joe" was what she called her jeep. She paused. "You don't think it's some kind of trick?"

"I sure don't—it's a little girl on the radio—I talked to her and so did Mary Lou."

"Is anybody else out looking?"

David shook his head. "Just Ronnie."

"Well, guess I'll start down at the old Caverness Road and work back—want to go with me?"

"Have to go find Ronnie," David said. He turned half around toward the gate, then glanced back. "Evening, Mrs. Beale."

"Take care," she said.

As he ran out the walk toward Old Shoe, David heard the jeep start and roar to life. Just like Donna—didn't waste time, she'd be on old Caverness Road before he got half-way home. Hurriedly, he unhitched Old Shoe and rode away.

His mother was on the porch waiting. "David!" she called out.

"Donna's looking, too, now," he answered.

"Never mind that!" And her voice had a frantic note in

it. "I kept calling on the walkie-talkie—Ronnie doesn't answer!"

"Oh, no!"

Bart Monroe snaked his eighteen-wheeler through the twisting turns of Rimrose, a small village eight miles east of Columbus, and shifted gears. Deadheading and light, he knew he could make it back to Birmingham inside of two, two and a half hours—except for this confounded rain. A few stretches of two-lane road, some four-lane patches, nobody much on the route, he could move it on. But a light trailer could jackknife on him too easily.

Well, he thought as he shifted into full high, nothing he could do about it. Ride it out, nobody waiting on him, anyway. Just the room in the big boarding house. He lighted a cigarette, flipped on the CB radio, and settled back. Traffic was dead but maybe he'd catch another trucker going west, pass the time of day—night, he should say—and routinely report no Smokeys on the highway.

Trouble was, channel 19 gave him only static, no voices, and after a couple of miles he decided to switch channels—maybe he could pass the good numbers to some of the locals, never knew, might come a time he'd need to know what channel they monitored, anyway. He turned to channel 11. Dead. He tried 12 and 13. Dead. Now, 14, he thought, lots of people hang out on channel 14. That one, too, was dead. He turned to 15, waited a moment, and was on the verge of twisting the dial when the static changed to the clicking sound he often received when a weak station came in. He turned up the volume.

". . . JBK 9119 calling, we have a ten—thirty-three. . . . We have a ten—thirty-three. . . . Does anybody copy?"

Bart had to think a moment, then he grabbed the power mike. "JFR 5155, the Dixie Bugman. . . ." He hesitated. "I copy you. . . . What's the nature of the ten–thirty-three?" He eased off on the accelerator so his radio wouldn't pick up extra engine noise.

"Bugman . . . Bluebird here." And Mary Lou gave all the details. ". . . All the lights are out here, no telephones, need the sheriff and a search party."

"Ten-four, ten-four," Bart answered. "But I'm a mobile, on the main highway." It was a young girl, he could tell that much. "But maybe I can relay . . . make a ten-five for you . . . maybe somebody'll pick me up, pass the message." He paused. "Which channel is the ten–thirty-three on?"

"Channel eleven . . . and please try."

"Ten-four . . . switching to channel eleven." Bart turned the dial back four clicks, gave a quick glance to make sure "11" showed up on the light. "Breaker-break . . . how about it, Bluebird?"

A moment's delay, then, "I'm with you, Bugman."

"Hang on, then . . . I'll see what we can do." He maneuvered a slight turn, then keyed the mike once more. "Break-break, we've got an emergency on this channel . . . ten–thirty-three on channel eleven. . . . Does anybody copy?"

Static and low engine noise hummed through the speaker, spasmodically broken by lightning crackles. "Repeat . . . ten–thirty-three on channel eleven. . . . Does anybody copy?"

Again, nothing except static.

He keyed again. "Bluebird, sorry but I can't raise—hey, wait a minute." He let off the mike key and stared down the highway. Half a mile ahead, where the road was straight, the shoulders wide and level, he saw headlights and made out two blinking glows that could only mean patrol cars. "Hey, Bluebird . . . we may be in luck . . . looks like a wreck ahead, patrol cars."

"Can you stop?"

"I can . . . and will. Stand by."

"Standing," Mary Lou said back to him.

Bart carefully braked the heavy vehicle and eased closer to the side of the road. Fortunately, the accident or whatever it was had happened on one of the segments where the roadway widened to four lanes. He eased alongside, downshifted, and pulled onto the shoulder just beyond the cars. As well as he could make out, a pickup and a small sports car were angled off the road, with one patrol car behind them and another in front. Bart put on the emergency brakes, turned his blinker switch on, and climbed down. No sooner had he put a foot on the pavement, though, than one of the patrolmen came trotting toward him. "Hey, keep that rig rolling—you can cause a serious accident here—"

Bart held up a hand to keep the flashlight beam from blinding him. "Wait a minute, officer, I need you."

The patrolman hesitated. "What's the matter—don't tell me there's another accident?" He waved vaguely at the two vehicles they had just caught. "Already got a couple of dumb-dumbs dragging on this wet road—"

"No wreck," Bart broke in. "Something worse." And he gave the patrolman a quick report.

"Oh, come on, now—how'd you get such information?"

Bart pointed at the twin antennae attached to his side mirrors. "CB radio—"

"Yeah, yeah, a Smokey report—"

"Mister," Bart said, "right now, all I can tell you is what the girl radioed. Can you come listen?"

"We've got this mess—"

"Anybody hurt there?"

"No, but it's hard enough to make out reports—"

"Reports." And Bart was beginning to lose his patience. "I'm talking about lives—a whole family. All you've got to do is tune in."

"We're not equipped with CB radios."

"I am," Bart said. He took a step toward his cab. "Come on, talk to her."

The patrolman looked from him to the cars, seemed momentarily uncertain. Then he hollered back, "Jerry, fellow here says he's got an emergency report on his radio— give both those drivers reckless driving and excessive speeding tickets—"

"What about the damages to their vehicles?"

"Make a note—let their insurance companies fight it out." He turned and followed Bart. "Fellow, you'd better be leveling."

Wordlessly, Bart climbed into the cab and turned up the radio's volume. "Breaker-break. . . ." He glanced at the patrolman and remembered that officers meant for truckers to use their call letters. "JFR 5155 calling JBK 9—oh, I can't remember your call letters, Bluebird. . . . Do you copy?"

"JBK 9119 back to JFR 5155. . . . I copy you, Bugman."

"Have a highway patrolman—"

"County deputy," the officer interrupted.

"County deputy," Bart repeated, "with me now. . . . Please repeat the nature of the ten–thirty-three."

"Ten-four." And very carefully Mary Lou gave all the details. "Power's out, telephones are down . . . need help badly."

The deputy reached for the mike and Bart handed it to him. He fingered it for the key. "JBK 9119 . . . this is Deputy Turner, Rodgers County Sheriff's Department. . . . What's the location of the missing people?"

The speaker hummed and crackled before Mary Lou came in again. "We do not know . . . somewhere around Rodgersville . . . one of the dirt roads."

The deputy turned to Bart. "Never can be sure," he said. "Kid's not certain—you know how they are, folks gone from home, liable to pull something stupid."

Bart felt like saying what he thought, decided against it, now was not the time to lose patience. "Ask," he said.

Deputy Turner keyed the mike once more. "JBK 9119 . . . Bluebird, Deputy Turner again. . . . How old are you?"

Bart's meter needle jumped, settled back. "I am thirteen."

"You're sure you're not trying some kind of trick?"

The meter needle rose, dropped back, fluctuated, then rose to a mark and held steady. And this time the voice was different. "Deputy Turner or whoever you are . . . I don't know how to use these radios but this is Mrs. Sam Gresham"—Bart sensed the edge of temper in her voice— "and there's no trick as you call it. . . . This is serious, a family's stranded and in trouble. . . ."

"All right, ma'am. . . ."

"Now hear me good, Deputy Turner . . . radio Sheriff Tate or go get him or whatever you have to do. . . . Tell him Mrs. Sam Gresham said get some people here . . . NOW!"

The speaker went static-dead and Bart stared at the deputy. "That lady meant it—know who she is?"

The deputy's tone suddenly changed. "Darn right I know who she is—everybody knows Sam Gresham's one of the biggest farmers in the county." He handed the mike back to Bart and hopped down. "Call her back, tell her I'm radioing the sheriff."

Bart couldn't help grinning as he watched Deputy Turner trot to one of the patrol cars. He waited a moment, then pressed the key. "Ma'am, Bugman. . . . That deputy stirred his britches . . . said tell you he was calling the sheriff."

"He'd better," Mrs. Gresham said. "Here . . . I'm turning this thing back to my daughter—to Bluebird."

Bart keyed the mike once more. "How about it, Bluebird?"

"Back to you, Bugman."

"Tell you what . . . I've parked my rig about a mile from the Rodgersville turnoff . . . I'll stand by . . . and I'm switching to channel nineteen. . . . I'll try to raise some other passing mobiles . . . sounds like you folks'll need all the help you can get. . . ."

"Ten-four, Bugman . . . and we'll keep channel eleven open for emergency traffic . . . may be a long night. . . ."

6/When he had reached the fence bordering the south side of the paddock, Ronnie had climbed the nearest post and dropped over onto the other side. The fence didn't exactly follow the property line separating the Winthrop farm from the Moreland place, but all he had to do was cross narrow Little Creek a few yards beyond, and he'd be in the soybean field.

When he got to the creek, he was surprised to find the water higher than it was supposed to be. Most of the time, a big step was all that was needed to get across. Tonight, however, it was muddy—and deeper and wider. He had to hunt one of the narrower places so he could leap across. He found the spot—near an old pin oak that leaned half over the creek—and used the jutting root knots as a platform. On the other side, one foot slipped and for a moment he thought he was going to slide back into the water. Clutching a small sapling, however, he pulled himself up and stumbled through the bordering stretch of scrub brush and thick vines. Past those, he was in the open field of thick, lush soybean plants.

At the edge, he paused a moment, half-wondering if he should have waited for David. David, though, had to find some other people to go looking. No point in doing that now, Ronnie thought, the camper wasn't that far away, just on the other side of the Moreland place, on that road the loggers had cut through the field last summer when they went down to the river and thinned the planted pines. He knew exactly why that Jane Horton's daddy had taken that turnoff—those logging trucks had made such a wide path up near the highway, turning right and left, they'd made it look like a real dirt road. Wasn't until you got a good hundred yards into the field that you could tell it wasn't a road, just a truck path through a farm.

And, he was certain, that's exactly where they were.

And he also knew this field of soybeans. He had walked over it more times than he could count, used to walk through it with David and Dad in the fall, when the undergrowth was green-brown, working the young bird dog, trying to teach him to hunt and point. Course, it didn't take long to find out that Jimbo wasn't going to do much bird hunting—David and Ronnie had made him such a pet that any time he got in the field, he thought it was just another romp. Dad had said they'd plain ruined Jimbo, but Ronnie didn't think so. Jimbo was lots of fun. But those romps in the field made Ronnie know all there was to know about this field.

Once, he stopped and flashed the light around. And in that brief moment, a flash of lightning gave a gray-green look to the field. And that's all he could see—a wide open field of soybeans—couldn't spot the creek-bordering shrubs behind him or the rows of pines and cedars on the far side of the field.

A moment of doubt caused him to stop for an extra moment to think. To his left—due east—and up the rise past the tree-shrouded vacant acres between the soybean field and the highway was the little community called town. To his right and maybe a mile or so west, the river was steadily rising—he couldn't see it, of course, but when the rains came like they were doing now, that's what it did—it rose out of its shallow banks and crept up and up, spreading out over

the bottomland till it flooded most of the soybean field—
and his father's eighty acres of cotton.

Mom, now—maybe she'd been right—maybe he should
have waited for David.

He shook his head. No, he was doing what he should.
He'd go on by himself. Just walk south in a straight line.
Get to the camper first. He could already see it in his mind's
eye—off the truck-rutted path and on its side, camper body
tilted, left wheels buried in the mud, little girl crying. And
he would be the one to say, "I've found you—and help's
coming!"

Just to be sure, though, that he was going in the right
direction, he took out the walkie-talkie, extended the antenna, and turned on the switch.

"Breaker-break . . . Bluebird . . . Bugman here. . . ."

". . . Bluebird right back, Bugman. . . ."

In the darkness, Ronnie frowned and stared at the
walkie-talkie. Bluebird—now that voice sounded like Mary
Lou. But Bugman—whoever heard of anybody called Bugman, wasn't anybody who lived in Rodgersville, that was
for sure. And no Jane Horton.

He tried to catch the message.

". . . Bluebird, I've contacted some mobiles . . . one's in
a Scout, I think he said . . . said he lived in Elkton. . . . Do
you read?"

". . . I read you, Bugman."

". . . A couple are on the way to Rodgersville to join the
search . . . tell the deputy when he gets there. . . . The one
in the Scout said he was going home . . . had some hunting
buddies with walkie-talkies . . . said he'd round up one
or two to join in. . . ."

"Bugman, Bluebird . . . that's really something. . . . But
tell me, is my signal holding up?"

Ronnie listened to the static a moment before Bugman replied, ". . . Hate to tell you, Bluebird, but it's fading."

". . . It's the battery," she said. "Getting weaker . . . I can tell. . . . Afraid it won't last much longer. . . ."

"Are there any other base stations nearby?"

". . . No," Mary Lou answered. ". . . Negative . . . only one in Rodgersville. . . ."

Ronnie heard nothing but static for several seconds, then, ". . . Bluebird, Bugman . . . back to you."

"Come on, Bugman."

". . . Like I told you, I'm near the turnoff to Rodgersville . . . still on the highway but on the gravel shoulder. . . ."

"I copy. . . . I know your location. . . ."

". . . How'd it be if I brought the truck over . . . use it as a base . . . if it's needed. . . ."

". . . If my base quits, we're in trouble," Mary Lou said.

". . . On my way, then, Bluebird . . . but how far?"

"Six miles," she said, "to my home twenty. . . ." Again there was a pause, broken by crackling static. ". . . I'll be at my front gate, flag you with a flashlight. . . ."

". . . Ten-four . . . JFR 5155, the Dixie Bugman . . . heading for Rodgersville. . . ."

". . . Ten-four . . . Bluebird down. . . ."

Ronnie shook his head. Oh, well, let them all come to Rodgersville, no matter how many, all they'd have to do was come get the people, he'd already be there because he'd find them first. He closed the antenna, cupped the walkie-talkie in his sleeve, aimed the flashlight across the field, and proceeded in the right direction. He *knew* he was still going south.

When he thought he had walked almost far enough, he turned the light ahead and flashed it all around. The beam outlined the trunk of a tree and he flashed it upward. It was a lone hickory right out here in the field. Now, that was strange, he didn't remember any big trees here. Only one like it he could think of was farther west, not too far from Dumbo Creek. He stared at it for a moment, then walked around it. He stopped once, looked back at it, then swung his light south. Its wide beam caught on something metal-looking. A quick goosebumpy feeling passed through him. The camper, right where he knew it would be.

"Hey, Jane—Jane Horton—it's me, Ronnie—" And he started running toward it. "I'm coming, I found you—"

He'd forgotten the fertile ground, the thick vines, and one foot got caught in the heavy soybean foliage. He tripped and fell forward. He was able to cling to the flashlight, but the walkie-talkie slipped from his sleeve and his free hand dug into soft mud beneath the thick leaves. He rose slowly and rubbed his elbow where it had struck something hard. It took him three frantic minutes searching before he found the walkie-talkie. And he was trembling when he flipped on the switch. He turned the volume all the way up. The static was still there, though not as loud as it had been earlier, but he couldn't hear Bluebird or that Bugman. He listened for a moment, then decided they just weren't talking, it worked all right. And even if it didn't sound as loud as it had, he wasn't far from Jane Horton's camper. She had a real radio—he could use that.

He trotted carefully the rest of the way to the big metal object. When he reached it, however, he found it not to be the camper. The field hands had left a disc harrow right where they'd quit working with it, out here in the open field.

No, he realized as he flashed his light around. Not out in the open field, right at the edge of it. For the soybean field stretched all the way to the edge, right up to a row of scrub pines and hackberry bushes. And it was south of the old logging road.

Slowly, he aimed the flashlight toward the harrow once more. A quick, numbing tightness caught at the back of his neck. His legs began to tremble. Wasn't where he meant to be. He was too far south, too far west. Couldn't tell which direction he had really come, which way to go from here.

His left arm shook as he raised the walkie-talkie, extended the antenna, and turned on the switch.

". . . Bluebird out. . . ."

Bluebird, Bluebird—Ronnie didn't want to talk to Bluebird, he wanted to talk to David or Mom, didn't like it out here alone. He pressed the "talk" button. ". . . David . . . David . . . you've got to find me . . . I'm lost. . . . Do you hear me, David . . . David!"

He let off the button, listened. Static crackled and hummed. He waited what seemed to be a full minute, then repeated the call.

Once more he waited. Then he heard David's voice. ". . . Bluebird . . . Bluebird . . . this is David. . . . Have you heard Ronnie?"

". . . Bluebird back to you, David. . . . that's a negative . . . repeat . . . negative, I have not heard him. . . ."

Ronnie pressed the button once more. ". . . David! . . . David! I'm here . . . at the far side of the Moreland place . . . across the soybean field. . . . David! . . . David! You answer me, do you hear!"

He listened intently. He *had* dropped the walkie-talkie. He could listen—but he couldn't talk back.

Wildly, he squeezed the "talk" button. " . . . David! . . . David! !"

Nothing except static came from the speaker.

7/N

ell Winthrop paced from front door to back, back door to front, anxiously staring out into the dark, trying to peer through the increasing rainfall—listening, wondering.

Riding Old Shoe through the night, David—she knew—would be safe as he pressed his search. Both boys knew the fields and woods of Rodgersville. Both knew the farm roads and the truck paths. David would follow a methodic approach to his searching, thinking out his route before going on. Ronnie, though, he was different. He would be plunging headlong, scrambling one way, then the other.

Out there in the dark, however, he would discover too soon that scrambling through open fields could easily lead him in the wrong direction. He had said on the walkie-talkie that he knew just where the turned-over camper was. Thinking back now to the excitement his voice had conveyed, she realized he was proceeding in a typically Ronnie manner—finding and hanging on to a conclusion, then moving headlong to convince himself and everybody else that he was right.

Nell's thoughts were suddenly interrupted by the heavy swish of tires from the opposite direction. She looked around just as a fast-moving vehicle pulled into her drive. George, she thought quickly. But even as the thought formed itself, the vehicle skidded to a stop and the driver leaped out.

Not George. Had to be Donna Beale, nobody else but

Donna would slam the brakes so hard, hop out and leave her motor running, her lights on. "Mrs. Winthrop," she called as she trotted across the yard. Nell realized then that the car lights had flashed on her. "Where's David—I need that walkie-talkie." She bounded up the steps. "Started down the old Caverness Road, what a mess, potholes washed out, water's over it in places—" She nodded toward her jeep. "It'll go anywhere as long as it's upright, but that road's too dangerous by yourself."

"David's not here," Nell said.

"Where's he—back up at the Greshams'?"

"I wish he were," Nell said. "But he's out on Old Shoe looking for Ronnie."

"Oh, Lordy, don't tell me he's lost!"

Nell took a deep breath and sighed heavily. "Donna, I— I'm afraid he may be. Started out, said he knew right where that camper was, turned off his walkie-talkie—David couldn't call him."

"God help him," Donna said. She turned and looked up northward, toward the Gresham farm. "Hey—looks like some cars pulling in up there—do you think maybe Mary Lou got somebody on that radio?"

Nell turned, too. "I thought I saw one a moment ago, couldn't be sure. As well as I can make out, those headlights tell me there's two or three, maybe more."

"Tell you what," Donna said, "I'll run up there—if there's folks come to hunt for the camper. I'll tell them he's missing"—she caught herself and turned back to Nell—"tell them to call for him while they're looking." She started toward the driveway. "Don't worry—those kids know those fields and woods like they know this house. Wandered off too far, that's all. They'll be home soon."

But as Nell watched her roar backward, spin the wheel, and head toward the neighboring farm, she knew better. Ronnie was lost somewhere in those open fields he knew so well—lost because he knew them in daylight but had no idea what they were like after dark. And David, riding Old Shoe, would stay out there all night searching. . . .

David had guided Old Shoe out to the highway—so he could circle the fence separating their farm from the More-land place—and just south of Little Creek; then he'd ridden back along the scrub brush on the opposite side until he reached the edge of the soybean field. He tried to guess just where Ronnie had crossed over and turned his light on the uneven line where soybeans met creek brush. If, as Ronnie had told his mother, he had a good idea where the camper was—and just how he'd come to that conclusion, David couldn't begin to guess—chances were he had just climbed the fence closest to where he'd been standing and jumped over Little Creek like they always did. But whether he'd done that or gone to the paddock's corner post didn't mat-ter—in the lush green fields all paths were obscured.

He turned the flashlight beam on the ground and ran it back and forth, hoping that his brother had somehow trampled his own path. Nothing.

At a place he guessed to be opposite the huge oak in the paddock, halfway between the barn and the gate, David paused, then turned Old Shoe in a direction that was as nearly true south as he could determine. He extended the walkie-talkie antenna and pressed the "talk" button. "Ron-nie . . . Ronnie, do you hear me? If you're in the field, answer me. Wherever you are, answer me. . . . Ronnie. . . ."

Maybe teasing him with radio talk would get him. "Do you copy?"

He released the button and listened. Static, crackling static, that's all he heard from the little speaker. Then, ". . . JBK 9119 . . . the Bluebird. . . . David . . . do you copy?"

· He pressed the button once more. ". . . I—"

A slashing bolt of lightning split the dark and struck somewhere on the river—or along the bank, David couldn't tell which. It startled him, and his finger slipped from the button. He waited till the thunder died, then he tried again. ". . . I copy. . . . Am on the Moreland place looking for Ronnie. . . . Have you heard him?"

"I can barely copy. . . . Come back with that."

David repeated the message.

". . . David . . . this is Bluebird. . . . My battery is getting too weak . . . I cannot copy you clearly. . . ."

David stared at the walkie-talkie, clearly understanding. He knew he had made a mistake, should have asked Donna to go to the sheriff's office; had no way of knowing, though, what Mary Lou would be able to do, had been so sure she'd contact somebody. But if she hadn't talked to anyone by now, chances were she wouldn't.

"That Ronnie!" he said aloud. "If he'd just stayed put like I told him to, I could find somebody else to go for the sheriff, do it all differently."

He brushed at the rain dripping from his hair and onto his eyebrows. No point in thinking that way now, though —Ronnie was out there, maybe heading blindly toward the river. He was sorry about the Horton family but Mary Lou and Donna knew about them—they could get the search going. He had to find his brother before he reached the river or got bogged down in the lowland that had to be flooding over by now.

He kneed Old Shoe, urging her to go faster, but he knew even as he did it that it would do no good. Old Shoe had her own way of doing things, ran when she wanted to, trotted or walked, as she preferred. He could spur at her with his heels hard enough, he supposed, and she might halfway gallop. But galloping through this field at night might not be too safe. Plowed ground always had its share of soft spots that rain could turn into sinking mudholes— and the one thing he did not need now was for her to hurt herself. So, impatient as he was to move faster, he let her choose her own pace. She stepped a bit more lively, though, when he kneed her a second time.

Four or five minutes later—he could only guess it took that long—he reached the far side of the soybean field. He could no longer make out the tracks the logging trucks had made but he wasn't surprised. They hadn't used the path in a long while, not since spring planting—their tracks had probably been plowed over. He stopped at the line of low trees and brush and aimed his light back toward the highway, east of where he was. Just at the farthest edge of the light's beam, he could barely make out the part of the path that ran up the slope and out the last fifty yards to the highway. He could not see through and beyond, however, because thick branches now overhung and shrouded it.

No point in going that direction, anyway. If Ronnie had reached it, he would have walked out to the roadbed and turned homeward. It was one thing for his younger brother to come wildly across the field, fully certain that the Horton camper would be on this particular path. It would be something else, though, for him to stop, realize his mistake, and deliberately pick another course. Not Ronnie. His excitement would give way to uncertainty, and that uncertainty, David knew, would bring to surface the old fear. Ronnie would head straight for the highway, turn left and trot home.

But if he hadn't done that, where was he now?

Again, he turned on the walkie-talkie, increased the volume. He heard bits of static but now it was broken by a radio voice much stronger than Ronnie's on the walkie-talkie, stronger than Jane's. ". . . Bugman here. . . . Do you copy me, Bluebird?"

A pause, then David heard bits of words that were blurred by the static. He thought the voice sounded like Mary Lou, but he couldn't make out what she said.

Then, ". . . Ten-four, Bluebird. . . . Is there a county patrol car in front of your home-twenty?"

This time David did make out Mary Lou's "Ten-four."

". . . Got it in sight. . . . Be with you in a short-short. . . ."

David did not recognize the man's voice but he understood the message. At least they'd gotten in touch with the sheriff, at least somebody else besides Donna would be hunting shortly. He halfway hoped some—if enough showed up—could help hunt for Ronnie.

He keyed his walkie-talkie. ". . . Ronnie . . . Ronnie, do you hear me? Answer me . . . answer me, Ronnie!"

When he let off the button and heard no reply, he had a sinking feeling. He knew that once Ronnie found he'd been mistaken about where the camper was, he'd turn the walkie-talkie on and try to let Mom or him know where he was—if he knew where he was. Being in the middle of the field on Old Shoe, David knew he would have heard it. Instinctively, he realized one of two things had happened—either Ronnie had dropped the walkie-talkie in the soybean field and couldn't find it, or he had dropped it and broken it—and didn't know it wouldn't work.

He pressed the button. ". . . Bluebird . . . Bluebird . . . this is David. . . . Has anybody heard Ronnie?"

He waited, then, turning up the volume. The static crackled and hummed—and a faint voice came back to him. He could not make out the words. ". . . Bluebird . . . Bluebird!" he shouted. "I cannot understand what you are saying!"

Once more, faint words, unintelligible.

Very slowly, he turned off the switch and collapsed the antenna. He thought for a moment, then steered Old Shoe in a westerly direction, toward the river. It wasn't supposed to be this way, Ronnie ought to know south from west, even if he didn't know the difference in the dark, he could stop and listen for the river sounds—didn't take much reasoning to do that. Trouble was, Ronnie didn't always reason things out—he simply made up his mind and acted.

Old Shoe seemed to sense the increasing pressure of David's knee digging into her side. Though she didn't break into a trot, David was aware that she stepped up her pace now as they moved westward.

Two minutes later, his flashlight beam picked up the disc harrow at the edge of the field. Too far west, Ronnie wouldn't come this far, he had enough sense to know this was too close to Dumbo Creek. Perhaps he had simply turned around and headed back home—

The flashlight beam caught something that wasn't all rusty-looking. David focused on it, stared hard, quickly climbed down and went to it. Even before he picked it up, he knew it was the bright yellow belt from Ronnie's raincoat.

8/

Outside, even though it was raining, the night was warm, but inside the darkened camper's cab Jane was wet all over, wet and shivering cold. Her whole body ached, her left arm was still pinned behind her father's back, its numbness now replaced by the needle-prick pains of a limb gone to sleep. Her neck hurt from the effort to keep it from falling against her father's shoulder—she kept it away because she feared that somehow, though she fought against it, she might go to sleep. The cramp in her leg was no longer simply uncomfortable—now she felt stabs of pain from the ankle.

If she could just put the radio microphone down for a minute and flex her fingers—but she dared not. Once her fingers loosed their hold, the small black object could easily slip from her palm, fall under her legs to the floor—and if it ever got out of reach she would be unable to recover it.

The only comforting thing was that now she heard other voices on the radio—Bluebird, whoever she was, giving the emergency message, and Bugman finally coming back. Twice she thought she heard David calling for Ronnie, but she no longer heard Ronnie. They were starting to hunt for her family but the thought gave her little comfort. She knew her father was hurt and she'd heard nothing from her mother since her first screaming out just as the camper toppled over. What frightened her more than anything else, however, was the changing sound of the rain. At first, she could make out the sounds of heavy drops hitting dirt and camper body and trees. Now the sound was different, like rain falling on a pool or a river, splashing noises. Somewhere close, there could be that river—or maybe a wide creek—something that filled and flowed over—

She squeezed her eyes shut, fighting back the tears.

And now there were other voices on the radio: ". . . Bluebird . . . Plowboy here, heading your way. . . . What's your twenty?" (Plowboy—you never could tell what kind of handles CBers would pick up.) Then, ". . . Plowboy . . . Bugman here. . . . Bluebird's power is not good but I copy you loud and clear. . . . Her home-twenty's six and three-tenths of a mile south of Route Eighty-two, State Highway Nineteen. . . . Do you copy?"—And, ". . . Bugman, Plowboy right back. . . . I copy. . . . will somebody be there to signal us?"—And, ". . . Look for my eighteen-wheeler . . . lights blinking across from her home-twenty,"—And, ". . . Ten-four, Bugman . . . at the turnoff now."

An eighteen-wheeler, Jane thought, a truck that big couldn't drive through these dirt roads, it would bog down, couldn't make those sharp turns—

". . . Bugman, you got the Catfish here. . . . Do you copy?"

"I copy you, Catfish . . . but we have a ten—thirty-three. . . ."

"Ten-four, ten-four . . . I'm joining you . . . but, fellow, I know some of those backroads, you try snaking that trailer into the woods, it'll take bulldozers to get you out. . . ."

". . . Negative, negative, Catfish. . . . I'm here to give Bluebird a hand . . . I've got power she hasn't. . . ."

Jane hadn't thought of that, but she readily grasped what he meant. Truckers usually had double antennae, at least a lot of them did, and strong radios—on the highway they sometimes came in stronger than the base stations her father talked to.

". . . Bugman, Catfish back to you. . . ."

". . . Come on, Catfish. . . ."

". . . Is the sheriff there?"

"Two patrol cars . . . deputies or the sheriff . . . don't know which. . . ."

"Ten-four . . . see you in a short-short. . . . Catfish down. . . ."

Usually, when she was sitting in the cab with her father while her mother rode in the camper, Jane enjoyed the way truckers and other people talked; often she didn't understand their special expressions but tried to make out their meanings. "Catfish down. . . ." Now, she'd figured that one out on her own—meant he was through with his transmission. And "short-short" or just "short"—that one meant a very little time. Her father didn't use that kind of slang but she was trying to make them all clear in her own mind so she could—

A low moan from her father broke the monotony of rain falling on water and metal. She glanced quickly at him, barely able to see him in the cab's darkness. "Daddy, Daddy! Wake up!"

He seemed to try to raise his head. It rolled to the side, held a moment, then slumped once more against the cab's wall.

"Daddy—Daddy! Mama—Mama!"

He was silent again, and no sound came from the camper bed. Jane squeezed the mike, pressed hard on the key. ". . . Bluebird . . . Bluebird . . . Bugman . . . Plowboy, Catfish, anybody . . . please hurry. . . ."

Bart Monroe had barely brought his eighteen-wheeler to a stop, hesitant to get too far onto the state highway's shoulder that might not support all the weight, and was just responding to Catfish and Plowboy when someone waving a flashlight came running across the yard toward him. "Hey, are you the truck driver Mary Lou's been talking to?"

Bart had expected Mary Lou but supposed she was busy inside. "Right," he said. Then, noticing that the man was a deputy but not the one he'd seen, he added, "Sheriff got the word, I take it."

"Sheriff Tate's on his way. Good thing you're here—her battery is about played out." Deputy Thompson looked up at the antennae strapped to Bart's side mirrors. "Looks like you've got a pretty good CB setup."

Bart had the best paired set of antennae he could afford and a full-capability radio. "It talks," he said simply. Leaving his lights on dim and his blinkers flickering, he opened the door and climbed down. "Okay to leave the rig parked here?"

"Well," the deputy said, "it's still partway on the road, but I sure wouldn't want you to flip it. Particularly," he added, "since the Greshams said you were coming to help."

"If I can," Bart said, and started across the road toward the large farmhouse, glancing along the driveway as he walked. "How many've come?"

"Those two," the deputy said, pointing to an off-road vehicle and a pickup with a camping body on it. "Together they brought six, all with walkie-talkies."

Bart paused and pointed at the jeep angled on the shoulder. "And that one?"

"Belongs to a girl lives up the road—Donna Beale. Would you believe—she's already tried one of the side roads."

Bart gave a quick chuckle. "Nervy, hunh?"

"You'll see."

Inside the Gresham home, eight men, a second deputy, Mrs. Gresham and Mary Lou, and a young woman in jeans —Donna Beale, Bart knew without being told—were gathered around the large kitchen table. Mrs. Gresham and Mary Lou were busy drawing lines on several sheets of paper, but Mary Lou stopped when Bart entered. "Bugman?"

He laughed. "That's what they call me—" He glanced at Deputy Thompson. "And JFR 5155. You're Bluebird."

"Ten-four," she said.

Deputy Thompson made hasty introductions but nobody seemed to be paying attention. "Donna," Mrs. Gresham said, "look—have I missed any?"

As Donna moved closer and leaned over, Bart realized they were drawing crude maps of the area—not to any scale, just outlines showing where the roads left Highway 19; how many there were, vaguely sketching in the turns and twists as they meandered toward the river. She started to make a mark, then suddenly looked up toward the second deputy. "Officer Cross, Lordy but I forgot—Mrs. Winthrop's worried sick, both her boys are out and she doesn't know where they are."

"That's all we need," Deputy Cross said. "Lost searchers."

"They're the ones who first learned about the camper," Mary Lou said quickly.

"I told her somebody'd come to her house," Donna continued. She glanced at the others. "Did anybody bring an extra walkie-talkie?"

"I grabbed what I had," one man said. "Got two little ones and a big thing." He turned to Cross. "You take it to her, tell her to leave it set on C-one—that's channel eleven."

"Will do," Deputy Cross said.

Once more Donna leaned over the maps and dotted in zigzag lines that stretched from the highway and across several of the roads, ending at the river. "Dumbo Creek," she said.

Just then they heard two more cars stopping on the drive. "That'll be Catfish and Plowboy," Bart said.

Heavy, boot-sounding footsteps crossed the porch and the side door opened. "This the right place?"

Bart looked at him. "You're Catfish?"

"Plowboy," the man said. "Me and Catfish both got two extra men."

Once more the side door opened and Sheriff Tate joined them. The sheriff, Bart saw, had to be six-six at least, and two-fifty, give or take ten pounds. He nodded at all the men, then looked at Mrs. Gresham. "Got here as soon as I could —what's the situation?"

Mrs. Gresham nodded to Mary Lou. "She did all the talking on the radio—she can tell you."

Step by step, without being flustered, Mary Lou told him everything David had said, adding her own information. A kid, Bart thought, but sharp.

Sheriff Tate shook his head. "What about the two boys?"

"Ronnie's lost, too, we're afraid—David's on horseback, looking."

"But nobody knows where?"

Mrs. Gresham nodded slowly.

The sheriff spotted the maps, took a hasty head count, made a calculated decision that put rural lawmen in a different light as far as Bart was concerned. "The drivers of those four CB-rigged cars, who are you?"

Plowboy, Catfish, and two other men in the crowd half-way raised their hands. Sheriff Tate looked at each, seemed to recognize only one. "Jeb Harper," he said. Then, "Okay, you four, pick a couple of men to ride with you—all of you have working walkie-talkies?"

The men nodded.

"Any spares, by the way?"

"We've got a couple," Catfish said.

"Have two in the car," Jeb added.

Sheriff Tate nodded. "Good—now Jeb, Catfish, Plowboy, and you," he nodded toward the fourth.

"Asa Perkins."

"You four, pick your men. Two of the others, I want you to go with Deputy Thompson. And you," he nodded toward the last man.

"Name's Jeffrey Gates—"

"How about you going with Donna—all right with you, Donna?"

She nodded.

"Good. Donna, you know all these roads better than the rest of us—I want you to patrol the highway, see to it the teams get to the right roads. Jeb, you're Unit One; Catfish —Unit Two; Asa—Unit Three; and Plowboy—Unit Four." He hesitated, then glanced around the room. "Who's driving that tractor-trailer rig?"

"I am," Bart said, and quickly explained his presence.

"Well, we're obliged"—he turned quickly to Mary Lou— "but since he doesn't know these roads—"

"If Mr. Bugman—" Mrs. Gresham started.

"Monroe, ma'am—Bart Monroe."

"If Mr. Monroe doesn't mind, Mary Lou can sit in the truck with him, she knows them."

Bart half-smiled and winked at Mary Lou. "Between Blue-bird and me, we can keep the radio going."

"Then let's move it," Tate said.

Mrs. Gresham gave each of the drivers one of the hastily sketched maps, holding the best one for Mary Lou.

"Oh," Tate said, "Thompson, take your two and run up the road to McShan—"

"That's east of the highway," Deputy Thompson interrupted, "and the little girl said they were headed toward the river—"

Tate nodded. "But she *could* be mistaken. Just check it."

"Yes, sir."

Outside and in his cab once more, Bart flicked on the roof lights and the smaller one illuminating the instrument panel. "Ever been in one of these before?"

Mary Lou shook her head. "Never saw so many dials on any car or truck I've ever ridden in."

"When we find the folks, maybe I can show you what they're all for." He flicked on the radio and adjusted a dial on the microphone. "It's a power mike—ever use one?"

"No, sir."

"Won't raise the output signal but it sure makes the voice louder."

"Any special way to hold it—"

". . . Mary Lou . . . Mary Lou. . . ." The voice was weak coming through the radio's static.

Quickly Bart turned a small knob, raising the volume.

". . . If you hear me, Mary Lou . . . it's David. . . ."

"I copy you, David. . . ."

A moment's pause, then, ". . . If they've started looking . . . tell them . . . please . . . Ronnie's really lost, too . . . and I'm afraid . . . afraid he's heading . . . toward the river. . . ."

9/B

art ran down the window and stuck his head out. "Sheriff Tate!"

The sheriff turned from the patrol car. "Yes?"

"Just got a call from one of those kids—"

"David," Mary Lou prompted.

"One named David," Bart added. "Said his brother was lost, may be heading toward the river!"

"Oh, good Lord—" The sheriff glanced off up the highway toward the Winthrop home. "And his mother has that walkie-talkie, probably heard him." He shut the patrol car door and ran inside the Gresham house. Moments later, he came out again, followed by Mrs. Gresham.

"Mary Lou, Sheriff Tate's taking me up to the Winthrops'."

Once more Bart stuck his head out the window. "Ma'am, I guess you'd feel better if I pulled my rig up there—you'd know where your daughter is."

Mrs. Gresham was about to jump into the car, but she paused long enough to glance up at Bart. "Mr. Monroe, doing what you're doing—I have a pretty good idea Mary Lou is perfectly safe."

"Thank you—but all the same, might be a lot closer to the searchers."

"Suit yourself—you know your radio," she said, and climbed in beside Sheriff Tate. The sheriff pulled his car forward, then stopped beside Bart's cab. "Radio to David that we're getting more men—I'm going to Elkton to round up as many as I can find. Lots of acres down there, soon be flooding."

Bart let Mary Lou call David and pass the message while he waited till the sheriff had turned around; then he slowly pulled the rig the quarter-mile distance up the highway till he found a wide shoulder just beyond the Winthrop home. . . .

Ronnie shivered and shook all over. Didn't like it out here all by himself, didn't like the dark, all that lightning, all that water in the fields, didn't like not being able to talk back to David. He heard what they said about his going toward the river, wasn't going that direction at all, river was west and he had already made up his mind he was going straight home. The others were out looking— he'd heard them on the walkie-talkie, probably the sheriff and some of his deputies were out looking, too, except he couldn't hear them on his walkie-talkie, they had different kinds of radios—so regular people couldn't hear what they were saying, he supposed. With all of them in cars, no use in his looking by himself, he'd just go on home and wait with his mother.

He clinched his teeth and drew his elbows close to his side. This field was nine acres wide—he multiplied nine by two hundred in his head, got eighteen hundred feet, then added two hundred just to make sure—two thousand feet. Divided by three, that came to six hundred and sixty-six yards and two feet left over. All he had to do was take six hundred and sixty-six big steps straight north, the way he often did when he walked through the fields with his dad, and he'd be almost to Little Creek. Counting those steps would make him keep his thoughts off the rain and the lightning and the vast dark field all around. He aimed the flashlight a few yards ahead.

One, two, three, four—

As he deliberately stepped big, trying to concentrate on making each leg stretch more than his usual pace, he tried to remember when he and David had been in this field last. Back in the spring, before they plowed and planted it. They had decided they'd go down to where Dumbo Creek entered the river. The creek spread out wide down there and Dad had said in that swirling water they could catch a string of bream and perch in no time.

Seventeen, eighteen, nineteen, twenty, twenty-one—

They had caught only one catfish, though—but it was a big one, measured seventeen inches and weighed four pounds—well, maybe not quite four, two and a half, Dad had said.

Thirty-seven, thirty-eight, thirty-nine, forty—

They had gone fishing half a dozen times since then, down at the back end of their own place. But for some reason the hooks seemed to get caught in brush and twigs and soggy limbs. They hadn't caught a single cat, just a few bream.

Fifty-three, fifty-four, fifty-five, fifty-six—

This field, though, hadn't seemed so wide on that fishing trip back in the spring, hadn't taken any time to walk through the unplowed stubble of growth to the mouth of old Dumbo. Tonight the field seemed a lot bigger—much more so than he remembered.

Seventy-nine, eighty, eighty-one, eighty-two—

Tonight, it seemed like he'd gone a full mile just getting across the Moreland field from the fence to that old harrow—

A lightning bolt split through the black clouds, its jagged edges looking like a giant, dull knife slicing tar paper. Right behind it came the axe-crash of thunder. Ronnie cringed.

Ninety-two, ninety-three, ninety-four, faster, ninety-five—

He knew the storm was now directly overhead, and not enough wind to move it along eastward. Just going to sit up there on top of Rodgersville all night. The river would rise, and the fields would be flooding more than they were now, and they were already flooding, he could tell by the way water seeped up and over his tennis shoes.

Ninety-nine, a hundred, hundred-and-one, hundred-and-two—

He was stretching for step number one hundred-and-three when his left foot got tangled in a root. He lunged forward with the right one and it just sank down almost halfway to his knee. Ronnie fell and sprawled out on the soggy soybean leaves. This time he dropped the walkie-talkie just at his fingertips, but the flashlight slipped completely from his grasp. He cried out and frantically groped about for it. Never mind the walkie-talkie, wasn't doing him any good, but he couldn't find his way without the flashlight.

He flailed and flailed at the dense growth before his shaking fingers found it. Trembling, he felt for the switch and pressed the button. No beam came from it.

He turned it around and held it so the light end faced him. He pressed hard on it but all he got was a dim glow. He squatted once more and, putting the flashlight as close to the ground as he could, he hunted around until he found the walkie-talkie. When he stood up and held it before him, he didn't need much light to tell that it was useless now— the antenna was broken off at the base.

Didn't matter. Couldn't hear, anyway. Maybe, though, Dad could take it somewhere tomorrow and have it fixed. He stood up and rammed it in his raincoat pocket.

Again, a blade of lightning slashed through the clouds and crashing thunder came with it. As its echoes died away, he had a quick thought about something his father had once told him. "If a storm comes, don't get under a big tree all by itself in a field—and don't stand in an open field—run for cover."

Ronnie trembled all over.

But then he clinched his fist and reminded himself that he had already taken more than a hundred steps. Wouldn't take too long to walk the rest of the way, couldn't run, might trip again and lose what was left of the flashlight. But if he counted faster, that would make him walk faster. He started moving, now stepping up the pace.

Hundred-and-seventy-five, hundred-and-seventy-six—

Almost two hundred, one-third of the way, just two-thirds to go. And he *knew* he was still going north.

Hundred-ninety-eight, hundred-ninety-nine, two—

He stopped, listening hard.

Water. Not rain this time, just water running hard, filling up and flowing.

He wanted to holler out *hotdog!* He'd gotten to Little Creek, hadn't been as far away as he'd thought, must have been taking longer steps than even Dad could take. Now all he had to do was find another good jumping place and he'd be almost to the paddock fence.

He bent over and aimed the faint glow of the flashlight at the water's edge. "Great day in the morning!" he said aloud. "Never saw Little Creek so full." He moved first to his right, then to his left, his spirits rising as he checked the bank. He found a place that looked firm and fixed, with one big rock that was wide enough for him to stand on. Funny, he didn't remember that rock. Probably, though, it had been covered with dust and dirt, rain had just washed it all off. Didn't matter. He could stand on it, make a leaping broad-jump, and sprawl clear on the other side.

He stepped up on it, waited till sheet lightning gave him an idea of how far he would have to jump, thought for a moment that even if he didn't clear the water altogether he'd be close enough to scramble out, then squatted one-two-three, and leaped as hard as he could.

Just as his feet cleared the rock, he had a fleet, panicking notion that this wasn't Little Creek. He hadn't walked north—he'd walked partway west, and this was Dumbo—wide old Dumbo, flowing toward the river. . . .

For what seemed like half an hour—probably no longer than fifteen minutes, he supposed—David rode Old Shoe crisscross over the soybean field, flashing his light, calling out as loud as he could shout. The rain, though, and all that thunder, they drowned his voice. Desperately, then, he pressed the "talk" button of the walkie-talkie, calling until he was heard, then relayed to Mary Lou that Ronnie was really lost now, heading the wrong way, he just knew. He had to tell her maybe toward Dumbo Creek—or maybe toward the river.

After she had acknowledged his call, he wondered and worried about the message. He knew it would upset Mom—

and he was sure that somehow Mary Lou or somebody else would tell her what he had said. He felt sorry about doing it, wished he hadn't thought it necessary. But riding all alone on Old Shoe, calling out and flashing the light about, he could think of nothing else to do. He had to act. Fast.

At the edge of Little Creek where it flowed into old Dumbo, he stopped and flashed his light up and down the washed-over bank. The soybean field didn't quite reach the water's edge—brush grew along the bank—and he kept hoping somewhere he'd spot one footprint, just one—anything that would let him know which direction his brother might have taken. All he was able to spot was washed-over rocks, rain-pocked mud.

Slowly, he guided Old Shoe to the south, backtracking Dumbo's weedy bank toward Park Road. Ronnie was frightened, David knew that, probably had panicked and was now running wildly through the fields, maybe into the woods that bordered the Moreland place on the south side. But scared or not, he'd have better sense than to cross old Dumbo. If he wandered this far, maybe—just maybe he had started walking south, toward one of the bridges that cross the creek along Park Road. All he'd have to do, once he reached the first one, would be to climb up on the road, head east toward the highway. But David could not depend on any maybes.

He continued moving slowly along the creek bank, letting Old Shoe take her time picking her way through the uncertain stretches where soybeans and the creek bank's underbrush joined in uneven tangles. No way to be certain, but he guessed he was within two hundred yards or so from the harrow where he'd found Ronnie's raincoat belt, about twice that far to the first Park Road bridge. Of course, it wasn't really the first bridge you came to along Park Road—coming in from the highway it would be the second one. Old Dumbo crisscrossed the road in two places fairly close together, maybe fifty yards apart, making a sharp bend south of the road, off in the woods of the old abandoned Clotfelter farm. Ronnie would know not to get off into that tangled undergrowth.

Lightning struck hard and suddenly, and it seemed to David that it might have hit another tree down by the river. Old Shoe reared up at the sound of the thunder that was like a dozen shotguns all at once and David had to grab the saddle horn to keep from sliding backward. He patted her, spoke softly to her, and gave her a moment to settle down before urging her forward. And in that brief moment, he flashed his light along the creek bank. Ten feet beyond where Old Shoe was standing, he noticed a barren place—no weeds, just mud and a huge rock jutting out over the water. Something unusual about the mud on the rock's surface made him stare harder. Slowly he climbed down, holding onto Old Shoe's reins, and walked closer. He squatted down and stared at it. A tingly feeling passed through him. Quickly he flashed the light all around, a tightness building up inside. There—and there—and there. Same kind of marks. Like footprints blurred by the rain but made not too long ago.

He stood up, flashed his light at the rapidly flowing and swollen stream of Dumbo Creek. He gripped the flashlight in one hand, the walkie-talkie in the other, closed his eyes. He had not cried in a long time but right now he couldn't help it. . . .

Nell Winthrop slumped at the kitchen table, the large

walkie-talkie standing upright just beyond arm's reach, its extended antenna almost touching the ceiling. She closed her eyes and cupped her chin in her palms. "He's scared, Cora—he's scared to death of darkness."

"Most people are, one time or another," Cora Gresham said quietly. "But think about it, Nell—those boys are like Mary Lou—they wander the fields all summer long, know the bottomlands as well as you do—maybe better." She opened kitchen cabinets until she found a candle-heated glass coffee maker, a jar of instant coffee, and two large mugs. She filled the pot to the center mark and lighted the candle. "I used hot water from the faucet—be ready in a jiff."

When the water was hot enough, she made two strong cups of coffee. "Cream and sugar?"

"Little cream." Nell shifted and stared at the walkie-talkie. Her hand slid across the table to it, and she turned up the volume, letting the voices come in over the static—

". . . Rover . . . this is base . . ." That, Nell knew, was Mary Lou, but who was Rover?

". . . Base, Rover here. . . ." "Rover" was Donna Beale, Nell could tell that husky voice anywhere. ". . . Units all in place. . . ."

". . . Unit One, base . . . where are you now?"

"Unit One right back . . . proceeding along Caverness Road . . . quarter of a mile in . . . road's pocked and muddy, patrollers are forward and on both sides. . . . Nothing so far."

Cora put the cups on the table and joined Nell, taking the chair at the far end. As she sat down, the motion made the candle lights wave and flicker. "Sounds like a military maneuver," she said.

"I wish," Nell said softly, "we had the whole National Guard out there."

"Base calling Unit Two . . . come in, Unit Two. . . ."

"Unit Two reporting. . . . A couple of hundred yards off the main highway . . . roadsides are clear but water building up . . . patrollers out and forty feet ahead. . . ."

"Ten-four, Unit Two. . . . How about it, Unit Three?"

The report from the third unit was much like that of the others. The vehicle was moving slowly along Landing Road but had to slow up for a washout and couldn't proceed until the front wheel locking lugs were adjusted to four-wheel drive.

"Ten-four, Unit Three," Mary Lou responded.

Cora glanced over at Nell. "Guess she and that Bugman are keeping them moving in the right direction—but lordy, where they get their crazy names from, I'll never know. His real name's Monroe, Bart Monroe."

"Whoever he is, I'm glad he's here," Nell said.

". . . How about it, Unit Four?"

A pause, then, ". . . Stand by a moment, please. . . ."

"Ten-four . . . standing by. . . ."

Nell glanced toward the walkie-talkie, waiting for the fourth report.

". . . Base, Unit Four reporting . . . moving along Thompson Road, brush is pretty thick on both sides . . . no room for patrols to walk along the banks, water's rising in places. . . ."

"Ten-four, Unit Four . . . how far have you traveled?"

". . . Sixty, maybe seventy yards. . . . Stand by again, base. . . ."

"Ten-four."

Once more there was a pause, longer this time than before. Static crackled as lightning flashed, this time farther to the west.

"Base, Unit Four. . . ."

"Go ahead, Unit Four. . . ."

"We picked up a weak signal . . . one of those boys. . . ."

Nell sat up straight. "Ronnie, it *has* to be Ronnie—"

". . . Said he thought he'd found his brother's tracks . . . somewhere along a creek, sounded like he said Dumbo. . . ."

Nell folded her arms on the table, bent forward until her face was buried. "Oh, dear God, no. . . ."

10/Sheriff Tate drove the ten miles from Rodgersville to Elkton, the county seat, in just under ten minutes. He had hoped that by the time he returned to his office in the old courthouse, the lights would be on again. When he whipped the patrol car around the last turn, however, and saw the square brick-building as nothing more than a dark silhouette, squat and desolate-looking in the center of the well-kept square, he knew it would be useless to go inside.

He drove about the courthouse square once, then, tires skidding, he headed straight for the center of the nearest residential area. At the first main intersection, he turned on his rotating blue lights, stopped, opened a door to light the inside of the patrol car, then switched the siren lever. Instantly, the screaming wail broke through the deadened sounds of rain, cut through the deeper rumble of thunder.

He kept it going, now and again adding to its noise by loud blasts on his horn, and waited.

After less than ten seconds, a sole flashlight bored through the blackness from a porch halfway down one of the side streets. Moments later, another and another. In less than a minute, more of them showed than Sheriff Tate could count. He switched off the lever, let the siren's whine die almost away, then revved it to life again.

And just as he knew they would, the people with the flashlights came hurrying toward him. His headlight beams picked out barefooted men covered with raincoats, some with their pajamas showing underneath, some in trousers and house slippers, some bare-legged. He could not see their faces, but he could imagine what their comments were, their mutterings about the sheriff having taken leave of his senses, rousing folks with that wild siren, this time of night.

As they began to close in about him, he flipped on the public address switch of his radio and picked up the mike. "I've got no time to apologize for the racket," he said. "We've got an emergency at Rodgersville and I need some volunteers." And in terse one-two-three statements he explained what was happening.

When he'd finished, one of the men yelled, "Who're the folks?"

"Ones in the camper are strangers—kid's George Winthrop's son."

"What kind of dumb folks would be looking for a camping place down there, a night like this?"

"I don't know," Sheriff Tate's voice was sharp and quick, "and I've got no time to wonder—I told you I need all the volunteers we can get—there's more than fifteen hundred acres on the river side of the highway where they could be. Got no time to explain more."

"When do you want us?"

"Now! Good golly, man—now!"

"What about the men at Rodgersville—"

"Down at Greensboro. same as all the farmers around Elkton. Now—do I get help or don't I?"

"Give me three minutes," one man hollered.

"Me, too."

"We're ready now," three men off to one side called out.

"How many do you need?"

"As many as I can get!"

"Have you got any idea how long it'll take?"

"Till we find them!" Sheriff Tate shut the car door, turning off the dome light. "Better wear high boots—river's up —and raincoats. Bring flashlights, extra batteries if you've got 'em, and if you have walkie-talkies, bring those, too— don't want any more getting lost down there." He switched on the ignition, then hesitated. "I'm going to pull out on the Rodgersville road, wait five minutes—you line up behind me. If you can't get ready that quick, come on as soon as you can."

"Any special place to meet you there if we're late?"

The sheriff thought a moment. "Yeah—when you get to Rodgersville, make a right on Highway 19. Up ahead you'll see a truck—an eighteen-wheeler—"

"What's a trucker doing there this time of night?"

A question like that didn't need an answer, but Sheriff Tate gave one, anyway. "Driver's acting as communications base." And he turned around and drove off before somebody asked what that meant. . . .

Mary Lou's hand shook as she handed the mike to Bart. He sensed the tightness in her arm. "You know that boy pretty well?"

She nodded. "David's in my grade—you see where they live and where our house is. Our closest neighbors. Have been since I was born."

Bart nodded. "I know what you mean." He took the mike and shifted the coiled lead wire onto his side of the gearshift levers. "Think maybe you'd better go inside for a minute?"

She glanced at him. "Can you make out the map if Donna calls?"

He looked at the scrawling and hoped he could. "Honey, I've been making out maps for six years going on seven. Run along, I can handle this till you get back."

"Be just a minute," she said.

"Okay—but leave the door open over there so you don't fall in the mud."

She climbed down, carefully watching her step, and scurried across the Winthrop yard.

". . . Unit Two to base. . . . Unit Two to base. . . ."

Bart keyed the mike. "Bugman—I mean, base back to Unit Two. . . . Go ahead. . . ."

"We are about three-quarters of a mile along Indian Bluff Road. . . . Those blasted Army Engineers have bull-dozed through . . . can't go any farther. . . ."

". . . Unit Two, base. . . . Hold a minute. . . ." He looked at the map but could not make out just where three-quarters of a mile would take them. ". . . Stand by, Unit Two. . . . Rover, did you copy?"

Donna's voice was uncertain. "If you're talking to me, what do you mean?"

". . . Did you hear what Unit Two said?"

"I did."

"What'll I tell him?"

". . . Ask him how far ahead the patrollers are."

Bart relayed the question to Unit Two.

"Unit Two right back. . . . About fifty feet ahead of me . . . waded through. . . . they don't believe a camper could have made it past the cut-through. . . ."

"Ten-four." Bart said. "Rover, did you hear?"

"I heard," Donna said. She hesitated a moment, then added, "tell Unit Two to backtrack. . . . I'll meet him at the highway . . . might as well move on to the old Ferry Road . . . that's the one I'm afraid they've taken. . . ."

"Ten-four, Rover. . . . How about it, Unit Two?"

"Unit Two right back."

". . . Return to the highway . . . Rover will meet you there . . . show you the next road. . . ."

"Ten-roger, base. . . . But if I were the people around here, I'd sure raise a ruckus with those Engineers . . . ought to have some warning signs posted. . . ."

"Base, this is"—Donna hesitated—"Rover. . . . Any reports from Unit Four?"

"That's a negative. . . . Why?"

". . . They're heading for the only high spot in the area . . . a little knoll, has some pretty steep banks a little over half a mile off the highway. . . . Might check to see how they're making out. . . ."

"Will do," Bart said. He picked up the sketchy map and glanced at the line marked Lookout—the fourth road north from Caverness. Unlike all but one of the others, it seemed to go about a mile or just a little more off the highway, make a curl, and stop at what was marked as a circle; didn't go on to the river like the rest. ". . . Base to Unit Four. . . . How about it? . . . What's your location now?"

"Unit Four to base. . . . We're coming to a slight rise, can't be sure but it seems like a dead end . . . no weeds to amount to much on either side, no trees. . . . Pretty sure that camper can't be along here."

"Ten-four," Bart said, then relayed their message to Rover.

"Okay," Donna said, ignoring the terms the others used.

"Tell the driver he's got room to turn around on Lookout Knob . . . but tell him to watch for loose rocks on the west side . . . they could slip."

"I copy, Rover." Bart waited a moment, then keyed the mike again. "Unit Four . . . base."

"Come on, base."

"When you come to the knoll, take it easy turning around."

"Man," Unit Four responded, "in this mess I'm taking it easy all the way. . . . Any luck from anybody?"

"That's a negative," Bart said. "When you start back toward the highway, let me know. . . . Rover'll take you to your next turnoff."

"Ten-four . . . Unit Four down. . . ."

In the radio silence that followed, silence broken only by the hum of static, Bart found himself wondering once more about people. No questions asked, no looking for glory, nothing but straightforward help.

". . . Base . . . do you copy, base?"

The signal was weak and Bart had to turn up the volume. "I have a weak copy."

"Lee Trotter with Deputy Thompson. . . . it's a wild-goose chase on the McShan Road. . . ." The man, Bart knew, had to be using a walkie-talkie. "Deputy Thompson wants to know if you've heard from Sheriff Tate."

"Negative," Bart replied.

"Okay . . . if he gets back before we do, tell him we'll finish this run then head back to Rodgersville."

"I got you," Bart said.

In the moment of relative quiet that followed, Bart half-wondered if anybody traveling through might be listening in on channel 19—the truckers' channel, people called it.

He had his hand on the knob and was about to switch when a stronger signal came through. "Base! Unit Three to base! Looks like we've found it!"

Bart keyed the mike. "I copy you, Unit Three. . . ." He grabbed the map. "What's your approximate twenty?"

"Little over half a mile off the highway . . . oh—never mind." And the voice had a let-down tone.

"Unit Three, base. . . . What is it?"

"Thought we'd spotted the camper . . . just an overturned shell of a car, abandoned . . . been here the Lord only knows how long."

"That's the way it goes," Bart said. He changed his mind, however, about switching channels.

". . . Tell Rover we'll go all the way to the river if we can. . . ."

"Ten-four, Unit Three. . . ."

At that moment, a tap on his door caused Bart to glance out the window. Mary Lou was standing beside the cab, a man's hat pulled down over her face and an oversized coat covering the rest of her. He opened the window and she reached a hand up to him. "Coffee," she said. "Mama said tell you she was sorry to use a fruit jar but it was the only thing she had with a top for it."

He took the jar and unscrewed the lid. "Rather have the jar than a cup," he said. "Holds more." He took a swallow. "You going back inside?"

"No." She scurried around the cab and climbed in, taking off her hat as soon as the door was shut. "Mama made me put this on—she knows I don't like hats." She shook her hair and brushed it back. "Nothing I can do for Mrs. Winthrop—Mama said you might need help on the map." She pulled some cookies from her pocket, unwrapped them, and handed him two. "Anybody call in?"

He told her what the reports had been.

"That old car on Landing Road—I know where it is—been there for three years at least. Maybe some day the county'll get around to hauling it off."

Bart nodded and was taking a second bite of the cookie when he caught the beams of headlights turning toward them from the Elkton road. "Mercy, looks like a parade."

Mary Lou watched them coming. "Sheriff Tate, I bet—looks like he got a bunch from Elkton strung out behind him." She paused, then added, "But if Ronnie's in Dumbo Creek, they may be too late. . . ."

11/In his favor, Ronnie was a good swimmer. As far back as he could remember, he and David had played in old Dumbo Creek, wading down it almost to where it emptied in the river, swimming in it when the water was deep enough. Across the Moreland place, where the creek went under the Ferry Road, the banks were wider than they were anywhere else along it. Right in the middle there, a huge oak trunk had washed down till it stopped upright. It was their diving-off place, though the dives were more often splashes and belly busters because the water wasn't deep enough for anything else. So he knew the banks and twists and turns of old Dumbo.

But not when it was wild and swift, not when it was overflowing its banks, spreading out, then dropping back and swirling. When he hit the water with the loose raincoat about him, he had no control of his arms and legs, nor could he keep the coat from spreading, filling, and carrying him headlong toward the river. But frightened as he was, and blinded by the frothy water and black night, he let himself drift long enough to pull his arms free of the raincoat and kick off his shoes. That, he had frantically thought, would let him swim against the current.

But even without the pull of the coat, his flailing arms did little more than splash uselessly in the muddy water. And kick as hard as he could, he found himself unable to raise his body to swimming level. He twisted and turned—

on his side, his back, on his stomach, on his side again, but he could not fight the turbulent rush of Dumbo, flowing toward the river.

Panic overcame skill. He tried to cry out but the grit-filled water frothed in his face, burned his nostrils. Believing the creek not to be too deep, he attempted to stand. Loose gravel and tugging water kept his feet from gaining an anchorhold. They twisted on boulders, banged against debris, slipped and caught and slipped again. "David, David, David!"

Swift water drowned the sounds he tried to make.

He began wildly grabbing at vines and weeds, overhanging limbs, clumps of johnson grass—anything. But his fingers slipped from the limbs, his hands uprooted the weeds, the thorny vines pricked so sharply he had to let go before his mind could balance prickly weeds against the unyielding certainty of the river beyond.

Just as he passed the crook in the creek where Little Creek joined it, he remembered the big boulder on the opposite side—if he could just get a handhold on it. But before he realized how close he was to it, his body banged into it and the increased turbulence coming from Little Creek pushed him farther toward Dumbo's center. Nothing now. Nothing but dark, muddy water, nothing to cling to, nothing to grab hold of, mud and slippery grass and moss-slick roots.

He choked on the water, his head ducked and rose and bobbled, his arms were tiring, his feet were dull weights, and all he could do was reach out and clutch, reach out and clutch, reach out and miss. His eyes burned and he squeezed them tightly shut. River. He liked the river when it was calm and softly rippling, fun to paddle the little rowboat across it, wedge it in the soft mud on the opposite side, drop his line over the edge and fish for cat that nestled in the soft bottom where the bank's elm and oak and cypress trees had large roots that made a natural fish sanctuary. River, he liked to swim in it during July and August and especially during the hot afternoons of September, when he didn't have too much homework, when he and David could make believe summer wasn't really over.

But he knew the river was now a wild, sweeping mass of rampaging water, giving Dumbo a ready place to spill whatever it carried along with it.

Ronnie cried out sounds that were neither names nor words, yells of agony and fear that rose up then faded in the muffling sounds of heavy rain. Pain-filled noises that reached nowhere.

As he swept beneath a heavier shadow, a flashing sheet of lightning outlined the narrow wooden bridge where the Park Road crossed Dumbo, but Ronnie was carried under it so quickly that he barely had time to reach for one of the undergirding trusses. His fingers slipped loose and all he got for the effort was a sharp splinter in his thumb.

He screamed out, then his leg struck a submerged log and it turned him beneath the current. When he surfaced again, he could see neither the shadow of the bridge nor its gravel-filled sides.

Another hundred yards, maybe fifty, he didn't know, never had counted the steps, just walked along it, he knew he would pass under the Ferry Road bridge. It was higher and wider, he thought wildly, and if he could just reach out to one of its thick posts on the left bank—just grab hold of it and he could climb out.

Fighting the time, not knowing how fast he was being carried along, he fought his way as close to the left as he could. His feet dragged in the sand and silt, his fingers groped for the rock and weeds, clutching at anything that would slow his progress, just slow down long enough to grab at the right moment. He didn't like lightning, every time it flashed he cringed, but right now he prayed for it to light up that bridge before he reached it, let him see where it was, maybe outline the road.

Sheet lightning came faintly from the southeast, thunder rumbled and seemed to last and last, but the faint light showed nothing of the bridge, very little of the bank. Ronnie guessed, turned as hard as he could toward the left, frantically stroking with his right arm to stay headed downstream, turtled his head as well as the rushing waters would permit, and stared hard. Vague dark shadows—nothing else.

Then he was at the bridge before he could get his left arm poised. He slapped hard at the support timbers but his fingertips barely scraped against one rough edge.

Knowing there were only two more bridges before he was heading straight for the river, knowing, too, that both were arched and high, with no way for him to catch onto them, he kicked and stroked and flailed away with his left arm, clutching, grabbing for anything he could cling to.

And just as the sky lighted up for what seemed like three long seconds, his left hand became entangled in thorn-covered vines. They pricked his flesh and he screamed but this time he fought the urge to let go. Momentum swung him to the left and his body was suddenly pressed against the soft clay bank. But miraculously the vines' roots held. With his right hand, he groped wildly once more, pulling at anything that would not give way. He brushed against a protruding root, held it, tested its pull, felt it give, and made a quick decision just to hold on for a moment.

His body pressed against the bank, his head and shoulders barely above the swirling muddy water, Ronnie gradually let himself relax. His nose burned and his throat was scratched from the grit he had swallowed, his muscles ached and his eyes, squeezing them as tightly shut as he could, kept filling with rain and creek water. He wanted to yell out that here he was, along the bank of Dumbo, just come get him, please, just come get him. But breathing was too hard, couldn't make a sound loud enough for anybody to hear, nobody near enough to hear, anyway.

The root he held in his right hand seemed loose, but if he didn't tug too hard on it, he knew it would stay fixed for a while—long enough, he frantically hoped, for him to catch his breath, for his heart to quit pounding and pounding.

He turned his head downstream so the frothy water would splash against his neck, away from his face, and carefully let his ear and cheek press against the muddy bank. Should have stayed in his own yard, should have waited for David, wished he had not heard that Jane Horton or whoever she was, maybe she was just somebody playing tricks, people ought not have those two-way radios in their cars, walkie-talkies weren't any good, just made noises—toys, that's all they were—toys.

Shivers ran through him. He knew people were out on the main road, some going up and down the gravel and dirt side roads; he couldn't see any headlights, though. They wouldn't come this far, they'd come a little way then stop and back out when they found that the water was rising over the roads.

Water rising. Soon the fields would be flooded, old Dumbo Creek would overflow its bank and stretch water all across everything so nobody could tell fields from creek. Vines would be covered, roots would be washed free, no place for him to climb to—nothing for him to reach for. Ronnie took a deep breath, coughed once, then screamed out "Help!" as loud as he could. The sound was caught up in thunder.

He shivered again and tried to dig his toes into the soft bank and wished as hard as he could that he had stayed in the paddock until David could walk with him over the Moreland place. . . .

When he had first spotted the rock where he supposed Ronnie had stood, David turned Old Shoe northwest and urged her into a near gallop. Couldn't be too far to where Little Creek flowed into Dumbo; maybe, he thought, Ronnie had just slipped in. If he could get to that bend where the creeks blended, before Dumbo made its sharpest turn and headed southwest toward the river—if he could just get there in time, maybe he could catch up with his brother—jump in with him, the two of them could fight the current, grab hold of one of the big rocks at the bend, climb out on the other side.

It took less than a minute to reach the spot, only seconds to flash the light about. Once, David spotted a brownish blob and thought it might be Ronnie, but when he fixed the light beam dead on it, he saw it was nothing but a chunk of log, broken off and floating rapidly. "Ronnie! Ronnie!" But his voice was drowned by the rain and swishing sounds coming up from Dumbo.

Without waiting, he turned Old Shoe about and headed

southeast, the way he had come. Riding as hard as he thought safe, he passed the rock and kept going along Dumbo's bank until he reached the place where it flowed under Park Road—the middle bridge, they called it. He swung left, let Old Shoe pick her way across the gulley that ran alongside the road, then guided her up and onto the road. Once there, he dug his heels in her side, urging her to trot. He wanted her to run, hurry hurry hurry, had to get there, but in the darkness there would be mudholes.

Still, it took Old Shoe only a couple of minutes to reach the third bridge. David stopped as they got to it and flashed the light on both sides. "Ronnie!" He listened. Nothing. "Ronnie!" No reply.

For a moment, he thought about riding north once more, upstream to that sharp bend. But if he did, and didn't find his brother, it would be that much time lost, that much longer for Ronnie to be swept farther down old Dumbo toward the river. At that moment, a crash of lightning forced a quick decision.

David quickly turned his flashlight downstream. Leaves and chunks of grass and shattered limbs bobbed and swirled on the creek's surface. A large wad of paper—he had no idea what a chunk of paper would be doing in the creek at this time of night—swept by. As it moved too quickly out of sight, he realized just how rapidly the creek was flowing. "Ronnie!"

He listened for an echo, a reply, some answering call. But his yell was caught up by the noises of rain and low thunder.

Waiting only a brief moment, he turned Old Shoe and guided her off the south side of the road, down to the soybean field once more. Keeping her as close to the creek as he dared, aiming the light back and forth as he rode, he urged her downstream in the direction of the Ferry Road bridge. Tightness kept building up within him as he proceeded. The farther southwest he went, the closer he was getting to the river. Ronnie couldn't be down there, down where the creek swirled and tumbled into the river, nothing to grab for, nothing to cling to. If he floated that far, the momentum of the creek would wash him well out into the river. Ronnie could swim across the river in daylight when the river was calm, David knew that. But at night and through the turbulence, which way was *across?*

At the Ferry Road bridge, he paused and flashed the light at the underpinning, the crossed timber posts that were built to hold the weight of fully loaded trucks. A good place to catch onto—if he had been close enough. But here, the creek widened, its rapid eddies moving from the banks toward the creek's center. He took barely time enough to flash the beam on the heavy posts, then guided Old Shoe up the rise and onto Ferry Road.

"Ronnie! Ronnie—it's me, David!" He listened hard, tried to hear any sounds that were different from rainfall. And this time he thought he heard one.

He fought the tremors inside himself and reined Old Shoe to a dead stop. "Ronnie! RON-NIE!"

He waited a moment. And this time he knew there was a different sound. He couldn't make out words, couldn't be sure it was a voice, but something downstream—how far he couldn't be sure—a sharper sound seemed to break through the rain's noise.

"Ronnie, Ronnie, Ronnie!"

Quickly, he guided Old Shoe to the left and down the slight embankment from Ferry Road and onto the wide field. And now it seemed that she sensed the urgency in his frightened voice, almost as if she, too, had caught the different sound. Surefooted as she usually was in broad open daylight on a dry path, she cantered in the direction the sound seemed to have come from. "Ronnie! Ronnie—Ronnie!"

This time there was no mistaking the answering frantic yell.

Sixty or so yards from the Ferry Road bridge, David's searching flashlight beam spotted Ronnie pressed against the bank, head soaked, hands outstretched, one grasping a clump of thorny vines, the other clinging to a half-buried root.

"David, I'm scared and I don't like this water and you better hurry and get me out of here!"

Before Old Shoe could come to a full stop, David was swinging over the side and onto the ground. Something slipped from his grasp and even before he could clutch for it, the walkie-talkie bounced once and splashed into the creek. Never mind, never mind, as long as he had the flashlight, never mind an old walkie-talkie.

At the creek's edge, he flopped down on the soggy bank and reached for Ronnie's hand. Fingers touched fingers, but as he edged closer, he knew he could not grasp his brother's arm.

He tried then for the hand holding the root. His palm touched the back of Ronnie's hand, but his fingers were not quite long enough to reach the wrist. "I can't, I can't," he grunted.

"Please—*please,* David—"

David started to inch farther, then realized that the soft earth beneath him could easily let him slide into the creek with Ronnie. Cautiously he eased backward and onto his knees.

"David, you got to!"

"Just hold on—I've got an idea."

"No time for ideas," Ronnie gasped. "Got to get out—can't hold much longer—"

"Don't turn loose!"

"Hands are slipping—"

"Don't turn loose!"

Wheeling about, David got up and reached for Old Shoe's bridle. He quickly unbuckled it and slipped it off. Clutching the flashlight under his arm, he took one of the reins and ran it through a stirrup, knotting and knotting it till he was certain it could not come free. Taking the other and holding it about his wrist so he would not slip into the creek, he flopped on his belly, put the flashlight so its beam came to rest on Ronnie's right hand. Inching forward till he was almost out over the edge, he reached down and wrapped the rein again and again around his brother's wrist, then triple-tied it into a heavy knot. "Now—now," he said, fighting to keep his voice low and reassuring, "work a finger around the knot—now another—now the others—no, no, not that way, grab onto it—there!"

"Maybe it'll slip—"

"Don't let it!" David commanded. "Don't you dare let it!" He wanted to sound less harsh but right now he sensed that he had to force Ronnie to use all the strength he had left. He put the flashlight on the ground, pushing it into the mud so some of the light fell on Old Shoe, with most of it still on Ronnie. "Now," he said, "I'm going to make Old Shoe move—"

"She'll pull the rein loose—"

"She won't," David said. "When you feel the strap begin to tighten, let your other hand slide slowly across the mud till it is real close—then grab the big knot with it."

"I—I'm afraid—maybe I can't catch it—"

"You can catch it," David commanded. "Do it!" He caught Old Shoe's mane, gently tugged it. "Easy, girl, easy —that's it, this way—whoa—now, easy."

As if she knew just what was expected of her, as if she were responding more to the words than the tug, she took one short step then another.

"The strap's cutting my wrist!"

"It won't cut," David hollered. "Just get tighter—but don't you dare let go!"

In the faint light, he watched the leather straps draw to a straight line, the stirrup stretching out with it. The bridle flipped and spread apart, but the reins held. David saw Ronnie's left hand move an inch, stop, move again, then slide quickly across the muddy bank till the fingers clutched the big knot.

"I'm turning—I'm slipping!"

"Hold that strap!"

Ronnie yelled out again that it was hurting him, that it was cutting his wrist. Without answering, David tugged harder at Old Shoe. "Little more, girl, that's it—a little more —easy, easy." He glanced toward the creek and saw that Ronnie was now up on the bank with his body no more than waist deep in the water. He thought it was enough but he wasn't sure and right now he wasn't going to take a chance. He patted Old Shoe. "Come on, girl, that's the way —come on, come on."

He did not stop her until Ronnie was out of the water and well up on the soybean-covered earth, till there was no way for him to slip back into the creek.

Ronnie looked up at him then, and in the glare of the flashlight David saw the agony on his face and knew tears were mingled with the rain and creek water. He patted Old Shoe, then turned to Ronnie. He was just squatting down when his own foot slipped and he kicked the flashlight into the water.

"David!"

"I'm here," David said quickly, "but I guess we'll just have to do all the rest in the dark."

Carefully, then, feeling his way in every motion he made, he untied the reins and slipped the bridle back over Old Shoe's head. He buckled it in place, caught the reins, and sat down beside Ronnie, still lying on the mud-spattered growth. Being big brother but trying not to let what he felt inside come through to the outside, he put his hand on Ronnie's shoulder. To himself, he said, "Thank You— Amen," then he pressed down. *"That* was a dumb thing to do. . . ."

12/J

ane Horton fought hard to stay awake, tried to force herself to listen to the voices crackling over the radio, straining to catch the words and directions. But the sounds of the radio were getting fainter, like a little transistor radio when the batteries were running down. ". . . Unit One . . . base . . . Lookout Road . . . Landing Road. . . . Base, this is Rover. . . ."

Moving out there somewhere in the dark, going up and down the backroads—and nobody knew which one to turn on. She wanted to say "Park Road, Park Road," but she knew now that her father had made a wrong turn, hadn't taken the Park Road at all, roads to parks were clear of brush. This one was nothing more than a truck path.

Didn't matter now, nothing mattered. Too sleepy to think about it, had to sleep for a few minutes, couldn't just stay there awake, just five minutes of sleep and she'd be able to listen carefully again. Let them get a little closer so she could use the radio, try to talk now and her signal would be so weak nobody could hear her over the other voices. If she could just get her left arm free, if the truck just had a different kind of seat in it, maybe those bucket seats that were a lot more comfortable. On the bench seat, though, she couldn't even slide up, and anyway, her legs were caught between her father's foot and the gearshift post, couldn't reach the glove compartment where the flashlight was, couldn't do anything but stay there and hurt.

She sniffled and called, "Mama—Mama," but the low sound, she knew, couldn't penetrate the walls of the camper body.

She just couldn't keep her eyes from closing.

Her body slumped against her father and those crazy wild half-dream thoughts kept passing in and out of her mind. Wasn't in the country, wasn't raining outside, they were riding through Virginia, all that rolling country, those pretty side parks where you could pull off and have a picnic lunch, and the ocean, some place called Marty Beach or Myrtle Beach or something like that, the pretty sand and the blue ocean with sunlight dancing on the whitecaps of the rolling waves. Not here, she wasn't here in these cold wet woods, rain pelting the cab and the camper body, splashing on the window, leaking through the partially opened window, everything wet inside, her father groaning now and then—

Wait!

She tried to sit up, tried to tune out the radio static, her senses suddenly and startlingly alert.

There it was again. Something moved, something shifted and the camper lurched and shuddered.

Somebody'd gotten to them, somebody had found them, the people, they were gathering around the truck and camper and in a minute they would open the door, somebody would crawl up on the hood and reach around and open the door—

When the camper lurched a third time, Jane knew exactly what it was, and it wasn't people out there. Soft mud, rain washing away the dirt they rested on, camper shifting like it might just keep going till it was upside down and she'd be on her head.

She pressed the microphone key and tried to holler "Help!" but her voice was little more than a whisper. Too weak, too weak. She was too weak and the radio was too weak and the camper was too weak and nobody would come in time—

". . . Unit Four, base. . . ."

"Base back to Unit Four. . . . Anything to report? . . ."

"Nothing. . . . Road's almost washed out . . . gulleys on both sides filling. . . ."

Roads on both sides filling—no, not roads, gulleys; Jane just couldn't keep it straight, couldn't be that many roads in a little old place called Rodgersville, couldn't be sure, maybe all those Unit Ones and Units Twos and Unit Threes and that base didn't have any idea what they were doing.

Once more she brought the microphone close to her mouth, took a deep breath, squeezed the button hard, and yelled, "Please help us!" as loud as she could, then let off the button.

She waited.

". . . Rover, this is base. . . . the sheriff has a line of men . . . moving south through the fields. . . . Has anyone heard anything from the camper? . . . Come back. . . ."

Jane's body shook all over. Her fingers clutching the mike trembled. Nobody heard her. She could not keep from crying. . . .

Mary Lou squinted and studied the map, ran her fingers over the scrawled lines. "They're not really accurate," she said slowly, "but they're all the roads going toward the river." She glanced up at Bart. "Could they be a lot farther away than we think?"

Bart rubbed his chin and tried to peer through the heavy rain. "Wouldn't think so—walkie-talkies pick up a lot of signals a good way off, but you can't transmit very far with most of them. A night like this, a couple of miles away is about all the talking range they'd have—especially to a mobile."

"Then why haven't they found the camper?" Mary Lou hesitated. "And Ronnie?"

Bart sipped at the half-empty jar of coffee. "Camper could have slipped off into some high brush, but if that little girl would keep transmitting—"

"She could be hurt bad."

Bart nodded. "Could be hurt, could be unconscious—could simply have fallen asleep. But with the mobile units making all the roads—and she said they were on a road—the camper'll be found." He stopped, then added, "The boy, though—that's something else."

Mary Lou stared at the lines on the map, studying the way Little Creek flowed west from the highway along the border between the Winthrop farm and the Moreland place, then tracing with her finger the route that Dumbo Creek followed—flowing westward through the viaduct under the highway, curling south and passing beneath Park Road, then bending crazily northwest and going under the same road a second time, moving through the Moreland farmland to where Little Creek joined it. She paused with her finger on that spot. "Creek gets wider here."

"And with all this rain, probably a lot swifter," Bart said.

"I've seen it when it wasn't much more than a little trickling stream," Mary Lou said, "but I bet it's roaring now." Slowly, then, she traced the course from the juncture, following the almost straight line southwest toward the river, passing beneath Park, Ferry, Thompson and Landing roads before it emptied into the river. "I sure wouldn't want to be out there tonight."

"Nobody does," Bart said. "But just look at the cars—must be twenty-five or thirty men, maybe more, walking through those fields."

"Didn't take Sheriff Tate long to round up a crowd," she admitted. "But those four mobiles—how'd you get them here so fast?"

"Lucky—just plain luck," Bart said. "Plowboy had been fishing, Catfish had stopped at some roadside café for coffee when the lights went out. One of the others had just put a new antenna on his pickup and was checking it out—and the last one just happened to be in his home driveway."

"Well," Mary Lou said, "if you hadn't caught them—"

"If it hadn't been me, somebody else would've gotten your call."

"Maybe."

"No maybe about it," Bart said. "CBers are a strange bunch—some of 'em, at least. Spend half their talking time asking for radio checks, trying to find out how far away they can talk—you know, ratchet-jawing—"

"Ratchet-jawing," Mary Lou broke in. "I've heard men say that but I'm not sure what it means.

Bart halfway smiled. "Just radio slang for talk-talk-talk without saying much. But"—and the smile faded—"you have trouble, they'll pitch in. Like that jamboree I went to in Memphis last month."

"Jamboree—that's a kind of picnic, I thought."

"In CB language, it's a way to raise money. Some trucker's wife had major surgery and didn't have the money for all his bills. CB radio people all over the county ran the channels, talking up the idea of helping out, printed tickets, got door prizes, gathered at a shopping center parking lot one Sunday afternoon and raised over ten thousand dollars for the woman."

"Ten thousand dollars?" The figure sounded too large.

"That's right." Bart said.

"Never heard of anything like that."

"Happens all over the country—in my travel bag I've got tickets right now for half a dozen—some call 'em jamborees and others call them coffee breaks. All the same. People pitching in."

Mary Lou nodded. "And like tonight," she said.

"Like tonight—"

". . . Base, Unit Three. . . ."

Bart grabbed the mike. "Base right back. . . . Come in, Unit Three."

"Did you copy a weak signal just then?"

"Negative."

". . . One of our patrollers thought he heard something on his 'talkie. . . ."

Bart reached down below the side of his seat and Mary Lou heard a low click. The radio volume jumped suddenly. ". . . Base to Unit Three. . . . If it comes back—by the way, was it a girl or a boy?"

"He couldn't tell . . . sounded like *help* but he wasn't sure."

"Ten-four . . . if it comes back, I'll pick it up. . . ."

"Ten-four, base. . . . Unit Three down. . . ."

Bart put the coffee jar on the floor and reached for his radio. He flipped two levers and turned the volume knob all the way up.

"What're those?"

"The switches? One cuts out some of the static noise, the other one's a fine tuner."

"Do you think they heard Jane Horton—or maybe David?"

"Don't know," Bart said slowly, "but if they try again, we'll hear."

Mary Lou turned and looked toward the Winthrop house, feeling certain that Mrs. Winthrop had not heard the weak signal but guessing she'd heard the exchange between Bart and Unit Three. "I sure wish it could be both. . . ."

13/E ngulfed in darkness, with David in the saddle and Ronnie sitting astride Old Shoe, his arms locked around his brother's waist, they moved at a steady pace across the soybean field. "Maybe it was dumb," Ronnie said slowly.

"No maybe to it—you know how those fields get when it rains so hard and long."

"Okay, okay," Ronnie said. "But I just did what I thought was right."

David was quiet for a moment, understanding the thoughts and fears going through his brother's mind. Without urging her on, he let Old Shoe pick her pace and path. "You could have waited like I said."

Ronnie took a deep breath and his sigh felt like heavy blowing on David's neck. "I—I know. But do me a favor, will you?"

"What?"

"Just don't fuss at me—not now."

David shifted in the saddle, easing off on the reins as Old Shoe moved right, then left again as if working around something the boys could not see. Slowly he shifted his hands, catching the reins in his right hand and letting his left ease back till his fingers touched Ronnie's wrist. He pressed gently. "Okay," he said, and he tried to make it sound gentle, "no more fussing tonight. Anyway"—and he tried to shift to a lighter tone—"there'll be enough fussing when we get home."

"Dad?"

"Dad," David repeated. "We're both going to catch it for losing those walkie-talkies and flashlights."

"You don't think he'll be too mad when we say how it happened?"

"No telling." David felt certain his father would not be upset with them, particularly when he learned the whole truth of it. Chances were, he'd think a while, stare hard at both of them and say in his easy-gruff manner that they'd better have a good crop of watermelons if they wanted him to replace the things they'd lost.

"But right now," Ronnie said, interrupting David's thoughts, "where's Old Shoe taking us—thought we were going back to the Ferry Road."

"We'll get there," David said. "Right now, it's easier for her to cross these fields. We'll let her pick her own way till we get to the abandoned stretch of the old gravel pit road—no ditches to cross. I'll guide her back to the Ferry Road then."

"Aren't we just about there?"

"Almost—"

Before he could complete the sentence, a long-lasting flash of sheet lightning gave everything a greenish-yellow glow. And in that quick instant, David reined up sharply. "Did you see it?"

"What?"

"There—through the brush on the other side of the old road—looks like something different." David felt nerve thrills pass through him, half-thinking he knew what it was, half-doubting it.

"I don't see—hey, looks like something turned over—"

Lightning again gave the field and woods a greenish-yellow glow. And in that fleeting instant, as both peered through the shadows, the bottom side of a vehicle showed like a half-silhouette.

"It's them—it's got to be them!"

David felt Ronnie's arm clutch hard about his waist. "Could be another abandoned car," he said.

"No car's here," Ronnie said. "It's the camper."

David felt the urge to dig his heels into Old Shoe's sides, pressing her into a quick run. He caught himself. Ten, maybe fifteen yards, wasn't sure of the surface, right now he did not want to force her into stepping in the wrong place. His knee pressure, though, seemed to transfer to the mare a sense of urgency. She raised her head, pricked her ears forward, and pressed through the weeds and tall grass to the rutted truck path of the abandoned road.

As they came nearer, the silhouette began to take real shape. The camper seemed to be almost flat on its left side, its left wheels buried in soft earth. Saplings were bent back near the body top but only tall vines were around the hood and cab. David carefully guided Old Shoe to its front, checking the reins firmly when it seemed that she wanted to shy away from the vehicle. "Jane," he called.

He received no answer.

"David," Ronnie whispered, "maybe—you don't think they're all—I mean—" He caught at the word.

"No," David said quickly, "they're not dead." He spoke with more confidence than he felt. "Jane!" He waited. "Jane Horton—it's me, David!"

Again, no response.

"I'm scared," Ronnie said. "Let's go get the others."

"I'll stay—maybe get her to answer. You go for the others—"

"No!"

Instantly, David sensed fear and quickened anxiety in that one sharply spoken word. "Okay—but we can't just stand here waiting. Here"—he took the reins and held them to the side and back—"you keep Old Shoe still while I look around."

"Don't fall in any mudholes—it's dark."

"I won't fall in any mudholes."

Dismounting, David pushed through the weeds, feeling for the hood of the truck. Slowly, he moved forward of it, toward the windshield. When he got to it, he had to push a broken plum tree limb back out of his way before he could peer inside. Crouching and staring, he waited for lightning to flash again. When it did, it came like three diffused backlights, one after the other. Not much light but enough for him to make out the form of a man leaning hard against the left door. Pressed against him was the much smaller form of a little girl. He couldn't be sure, but it looked almost like she was asleep, with her head resting on the man's shoulder. David thumped the windshield once, then gave it several hard knuckle raps. "Jane!" he hollered. "Jane Horton!"

Again, lightning filled the sky and this time he was glad it kept the fields and woods lighted for several seconds. He saw her head move, saw it turn. "Jane!"

The lightning died and he could see no more. But a breaking voice responded with, "Daddy! Daddy, somebody's found us!"

"Jane," David hollered again, "it's me—David. Remember—David!" He waited before adding, "Do you hear me!"

The voice was muffled but he made out, "David, I hear."

"Jane—listen—do you have a flashlight? A *flashlight?*"

"In the—the glove compartment—but I can't reach it."

David couldn't be sure, but he thought her head slumped against the man's shoulder again. He stood quickly and turned to Ronnie and Old Shoe. "She's almost unconscious —can't talk much." He scurried around the hood and front of the truck once more.

"What are you going to do?" Ronnie asked.

"Got to get inside somehow." He climbed back on Old Shoe and steered her to the bottom-side of the camper. At the door, he stood in the stirrups and leaned forward.

"What're you doing?"

"Got to get the door open." He stretched, caught the handle, and pulled himself up till he was lying on the camper's side. Spreading his legs so he wouldn't slide off the wet surface, he turned the handle. It clicked but he could not lift the door. "Can't."

"What's the matter?"

"Door's too heavy."

"No wonder—truck doors are heavy, don't you know that?"

Without answering, David eased off and felt with his legs until he was astride Old Shoe again. He thought a minute then kneed Old Shoe till she was almost touching the camper's underside.

"Now what?" Ronnie asked.

"If I stand, I can get it partway open. You reach under-neath and crank the window."

"Suppose you can't hold it—I don't want my arm caught—"

"I can hold it," David said quickly. He bent over and turned the handle. When its latch clicked free, he strained with his right arm until he could grip the door's edge with his left hand. Grunting and stretching, he got it up high enough to prop it with his elbow and forearm. "Now!" he said. "Grab that crank and turn it."

Together they struggled until Ronnie got his fingers on the crank. Turning it was a slow process because he couldn't get a full grip, but when the next flare of sheet lightning brightened the sky they both saw that the window was open. "Enough," David said. "Now get your arm out of the way."

When Ronnie's hand was clear of the door's edge, David slowly let the weight down till his fingers were almost wedged in the crack. He jerked them free and let the door close. "Got it," he said. Once more he stretched and pulled himself onto the camper's side, again spreading his legs. He slid forward till his body was partway over the window opening. "Jane—Jane Horton! Wake up! WAKE UP!"

He vaguely watched the shadow move, the head lift off her father's shoulder. "Somebody, somebody."

"It's me—David. DAVID!"

She choked and he thought she was about to cry. "Get us out."

"We need more help," he said. "Lots more."

"Help," she echoed.

"Jane—Jane! Wake up—do you understand me—WAKE UP!"

Her sigh was heavy and hoarse. "I—I think so."

"We need your flashlight—I'll try to get it." He inched forward over the door, his left shoulder partially covering the window's opening. He stretched forward inches more, reaching until he found the glove compartment button. He pressed it, opened the door, and extended his fingers as far inside as he could. He felt about until he found the flash-light. When he turned it on, the light was dim but it gave a clear yellow glow inside the cab. He aimed it at her. "Use the radio—"

"Can't," she almost whispered now. "Too hoarse."

David remembered the microphone on Mary Lou's radio, the coiled cord like the one on the telephone that could stretch two or three times its seeming length. "Will the mike reach this far?"

"I—I think so." She reached toward him with her right hand, the mike still clutched in her fingers. "But I can't get it that far."

David squirmed partway into the window opening.

"David!" Ronnie's voice was almost shrill. "What're you doing? You're going to fall in!"

David paused, realizing he was barely balancing at the window's edge. "Where's Old Shoe?"

"Right here—where else do you think she is—"

"Get her close to the camper," David hollered back.

"She can't do anything—"

"Just get her close enough for you to grab my leg—hold it real tight."

"What good'll that do?"

"Just *do* it!"

He waited till he felt his brother's hand on his ankle, guessed by the firm pressure that Ronnie was holding the foot with both hands. Ronnie might sometimes be too quick to do things, might not always think things through—but one thing about him, he was strong. David felt his legs pressed down, knew he would slip no farther. "Now," he said, "Jane—Jane, do you hear me?"

"I'm awake," she said softly.

He turned the flashlight so its glow caught her hand, the mike, and his outstretched fingers. "Give it to me—that's it, little farther—just a little more."

"I can't—"

"You have to!"

She bent as far toward him as she could, crying out at a pain he did not know she was experiencing. But she swallowed the sound and turned as far as she could. "Can't get it any closer."

David felt a catch in his right shoulder as he twisted but he forced himself to extend the hand an inch, two inches nearer. Fingertips touched the cord, one finger wrapped itself into one of the coil loops and very carefully he closed his hand about it until their fingers came together. As if she knew exactly what he expected her to do, Jane gradually eased off while his palm flattened out and took the mike from her. "Got it," he said. He struggled back till he had his body balanced at the window's edge. "Never used one of these."

"It's easy." Jane's voice was barely above a whisper. "Just press the thing on the side—"

"Like a walkie-talkie key?" He thought he understood —he'd half-watched Mary Lou earlier when she was trying to call for help.

"Yes," she said. "Hold it close to your mouth, a little to the side."

"David!" Ronnie hollered. "What're you doing?"

"Getting ready to call for help on the radio."

"Well, hurry it up, will you—my arms are getting tired!"

David pressed the mike key once and it slipped. He took a

firmer grip and pressed again, holding the mike as close as he remembered Mary Lou doing. "Mary Lou . . . Mary Lou . . . this is David. . . . Do you copy?"

The sound came through Bart's radio in broken crackles, partially blurred by the sound of one of the patrols on his walkie-talkie. But it was enough for Bart to catch its meaning. Mary Lou sat forward and the map fell from her lap. "David," she said.

Bart raised the mike and keyed it. No time now to follow radio procedures. "Rover, all units . . . all patrols . . . stand by, *stand by!*"

The radio's signal meter needle dropped down till it was just above the number 3 and no sounds came from the speaker except the hum and crackle of static. Bart keyed the mike once more. "David . . . this is Bugman. . . . We copy. . . . Talk as loud as you can. . . . What's the message?"

The speaker was silent except for a low hum. Then, "Bugman . . . David here. . . . I found Ronnie . . . and we found the camper."

Mary Lou trembled and Bart felt the vibration through the seat cushion. "Shhh," he said, then, "David . . . Bugman right back. . . . I copy. . . . You have found your brother and the camper. . . . Can you give their condition?"

Again a pause, and while he waited Bart turned the volume all the way up. "Ronnie's all right . . . people here need help bad."

Mary Lou grabbed for the map. "But where?"

Again Bart keyed the mike. "David, what's your ten-twenty—"

"He might not understand the code."

Bart nodded. "David, what's your location? Your location?"

"At the camper . . . it is . . ." his voice faded.

"Where, David, *where!*" Bart hollered into the mike.

A moment's silence, then, "The abandoned stretch of Gravel Pit Road . . . forty or fifty yards southwest . . . of where it crosses Ferry Road. . . . Need lots of help and . . ."

Once more the voice blurred and both Bart and Mary Lou suspected that the camper radio was fading. Mary Lou ran her finger over a scrawled line on the map, touched the point of intersection. "Here," she said. "Right here—and Donna knows right where it is."

Bart keyed the mike. "Rover . . . Rover, did you hear?"

". . . Heard something . . . not all."

"David has Ronnie," Bart said, ". . . and he's located the camper." He looked at the map in Mary Lou's hand, then gave the location just as David had reported it. . . .

14/D

avid felt the door handle dig into his stomach and knew a cramp was beginning to tighten his shoulder muscles. Yet he dared not move, dared not take a chance with the mike—one slip and he would have no further way of relaying any necessary messages.

"What did they say?" Ronnie hollered.

"Said they were on the way," David called back. He let the flashlight play across Jane's body, toward her father, gradually moved it toward his shoulder and face. The man's head was resting against the cab's side, and David wasn't sure but he thought there was a trickle of blood on his forehead. "Has he moved any?"

"Once," Jane said and her voice was beginning to break once more. "You don't think he's—"

"No," David said quickly, almost harshly, guessing what she was asking but hadn't wanted to put into words. "Just knocked out." He swept her with the light. "How about you—any cuts you know of?"

"My shoulder's numb, arm hurts all over," she said. "My foot's caught, too."

"Just take it easy." David tried to make his voice sound reassuring. "They'll be here—"

"David! Here they come—lights bobbing like crazy!" Ronnie yelled. "It's got to be Donna, wouldn't anybody else come flying down that road like she does."

No, David thought, nobody else. Donna knew these fields and roads better, he supposed, than just about anybody else in Rodgersville. He couldn't see the lights, didn't care to raise his body from the position half into the camper's cab. But he heard the harsh roar of the motor, and when she slammed the brakes and twisted off the Ferry Road onto this abandoned stretch of the old Gravel Pit path, the bouncing reflection of her headlights threw a faint gleam through the cab's windshield. "First ones are here," he told Jane.

Donna skidded to a stop and David heard Old Shoe snort as she shied away. Must be mighty close.

"It's Donna, all right," Ronnie hollered. "Hey, Donna— here! David's up on the camper's side."

David heard both doors open and slam shut and guessed somebody was with her. He made out the sound of running footsteps toward the camper, and a bright flashlight beam cut through the semidarkness. "David, are they hurt bad?"

"Can't tell," he said. "Jane's wedged against her father, looks like he's unconscious—maybe pinned against the side door."

Donna scrambled around the front of the camper and aimed her light through the windshield toward the driver. "Oh, good Lord! Jeffrey"—that must be the man with her, David guessed—"go around to the back—David, have you tried to open the back door?"

"No," he hollered, "had to get to the radio first."

"Does the camper have a side window?"

"I—I think so, didn't really look."

The man with Donna pushed his way through the underbrush and pine saplings and David heard them brush against the camper roof and rear. "Door's blocked with briars and trees."

David heard another car and another, then more than he could count as doors slammed open and men began calling to him and Donna. "David," a voice called—Sheriff Tate. "How's it look?"

Before he could reply, Donna answered for him.

"Anybody in the camper?"

"My mother and my dog," Jane said. But her voice didn't carry and David had to relay the message.

And now there were more voices and scraping sounds. "Boy, we *sure* are glad to see you." David knew Sheriff Tate was talking to Ronnie.

"Yes, sir—we're glad to see you, too." That, David guessed, was Ronnie's way of getting attention away from himself.

"Some of you start clearing that brush—anybody got an axe?"

"I've got a hatchet, sheriff," one man called back.

"Get it—the rest of you start trampling everything!"

Old Shoe whinnied and snorted, and David heard Ronnie say, "Whoa—easy, easy there, girl."

"No need to hold my feet any longer," David said.

Immediately Ronnie let go. "I'm glad—arms are sure tired."

David reached down and handed the mike to Jane. "Don't need it any longer," he said. After he'd said it, he realized how unnecessary the remark was.

"David," Sheriff Tate called.

He caught the edge of the door, pushed himself up and out of the window again, and twisted about. He raised his head and was suddenly caught in the glares of car lights and flashlights. Couldn't count them all but there had to be thirty people, maybe fifty. "Yes, sir?"

"Can you turn around, look in the camper window?"

"Think so." Very gingerly, he grasped the upper edge

of the camper body, pulled himself to the left, and shifted his body so he was flat on the camper's side. Cautiously he inched toward the rear, easing the flashlight into his left hand. At the window, he aimed the gleam inside but the light was too dim to make out anything. "Light's not good enough—need a stronger one."

Somebody—David couldn't tell who—stretched up and handed him a powerful lantern light. David let go of the little one he'd gotten from Jane and it rolled to the ground. The third one he and Ronnie had lost tonight. Oh, well, couldn't worry about that now. He turned the powerful beam of the lantern through the narrow window and it seemed to illuminate all of the camper's inside. He swept the area, then carefully worked it about. Something seemed to be moving inside, and when he focused the beam on it he spotted a brownish young dog jumping up and down but making no sound. "Funny," he called, "little dog's all right but he's not barking—"

"Can't bark," Jane tried to call to him. "It's a basenji."

Somewhere, David had read about a little dog that could not bark but this was the first one he'd seen.

"How about the woman?" Sheriff Tate asked.

Again, David moved the light about. For a moment, it seemed that he could find nothing but a scattered array of boxes and towels, sheets and clothing. Then he spotted what appeared to be hair and he fixed the beam on it. Now he could barely make out the woman's head and he guided the light along a path that should be her body. She was stretched out against the camper's far side but he couldn't tell whether or not she was pinned. "On the far side, under junk," he said.

"Close to the back door?"

"No, sir—but the little dog is."

By now the brush and briars had been cleared away and David felt the camper body shake as some of the men turned the door latch and began tugging it open.

"Wait!" he hollered. "Don't let the little dog get out!" And he aimed the light on the animal so they could see it clearly. When the door opened slightly, Donna—naturally, it would be Donna—deftly caught the little fellow and tucked her arms around it.

"Tell Jane," she called out, "I'll see to her pet."

That, David knew, she would do. He relayed the message, then fixed the light beam on the inside once more. And now other flashlights were playing along the inside, flooding it with eerie glows.

Very cautiously, one man stepped inside, crouching to keep from bumping his head on the upper side of the camper. And, as David held his light on the door, he saw Sheriff Tate's head poke inside. The man within gingerly moved a cardboard box and some bundles of cloth in a place David couldn't see clearly. But when they were out of the way, he saw Jane's mother lying on her side, one leg crooked up and the foot twisted. "Looks like she might have a broken leg or ankle."

"Can't tell about her back, either," the sheriff said.

"How about the driver?" somebody hollered. "Water's getting deeper over here."

"Got to get the woman first," Tate said. "Have to raise the camper to get him."

David flexed his tired arms and looked around at the still-gathering crowd. Some were standing back, as if waiting to be told what to do, while others were busily trampling more brush and weeds around the camper. He couldn't help thinking that here all these people were, out in the rain and mud, helping a family none of them knew. Gave him a quick, good feeling—just being a part of it all.

"Sheriff"—and again it was a voice David didn't recognize —"we ought to have some kind of stretcher—"

"Don't have any—"

"I've got two fold-up army cots in my truck," another volunteered.

"Good—get 'em set up. Bring one to the back, here— we'll put the woman on it."

Flashlight beams cut wierd arcs through the night and sheet lightning, now well to the east, again gave the whole area that strange greenish-yellow glow.

It took only minutes to get one of the cots opened and stretched out. Four men brought it to the camper's door and one stepped inside with the man already there. While they were working the cot to where they could put Mrs. Horton on it, Sheriff Tate hurried to the roadway. "Soon's we get her out we'll have to raise the camper—"

"No trouble," Donna said. "My jeep's got a front-end winch."

"We'll need that," the sheriff said. "But how can you get the cable to it—"

Before he could finish his question, Donna said, "Simple—that big oak yonder"—it was on the other side of the abandoned road, David remembered—"we'll run the cable around it, bring the hook over the cab, and grab onto the underside."

"Right—let's get to it."

Donna led two men to the winch and aimed a flashlight at the cable hook. "As soon as I get the motor started and let off the drum clutch, you pull the cable. Carry it"—she aimed the light now toward the tree—"yonder. Looks like a sturdy branch about seven feet up—be a good idea if you could get it over that so the cable won't slip."

"Got you," one of the men said. He and the second one —and they were joined by two others—caught the hook and waited for Donna to give them slack. Dragging the cable, they made their way through the muck and brush toward the oak. When they got to it, however, they found that the limb she'd pointed to was too small and the first big one was about a foot higher. "Can't quite reach it."

"Need to use it," Donna said.

David sidled and slid around so he could watch. Ronnie was in the middle of the abandoned road, still keeping Old Shoe under control. "Ronnie," he called out, "maybe you can ride Old Shoe to the tree, stand up in the stirrups and get the cable up there."

"Don't know if I can reach it."

"You can try," David said.

"All right," Ronnie said slowly, "but I'm getting real tired."

"I know," David said softly, "but maybe if you just try."

"Okay."

Bathed in the flashlights and car's headlight beams, Ronnie slowly guided Old Shoe to the far side of the road and to the tree. When the men handed him the hook, he caught it and pulled at the cable. "Not quite long enough," he said.

"Here, let's give him more slack," and the four men pulled at the cable until they had an extra four feet of it; then they held onto the rest and raised it so the dead weight would not pull at Ronnie's arms. Ronnie clutched the hook in his right hand and guided Old Shoe as close to the tree as he could. Right under the heavy branch, he caught the saddle horn, stretched high, and swung the hook upward. It hit a twig he had not seen and slipped back.

"Watch it!"

Ronnie had to duck to keep the heavy hook from striking his face. He eased into the saddle once more and gripped the cable right where it joined the hook. And this time when he stood and swung it up, it went over the limb. As soon as he saw it dangling, he grabbed it and pulled hard, dropping to the saddle once more.

"Good boy," one of the men hollered. He took the hook from Ronnie, and the four then struggled until they had the cable back across the road and dangling over the cab's edge.

David looked hard at Ronnie, trying to see the expression on his face. Tired, that was an understatement—worn-out-and-ready-to-drop would be more like it, all that fighting the creek, running over the fields—and now this.

The men eased the cot with Mrs. Horton on it out of the camper's rear door. "Careful," Sheriff Tate said. "Got to get her to the hospital."

"Sheriff," called one of the men.

"Yeah, Art?"

"My camper sleeps two—put her in it."

"Right—some of you others help."

As soon as they had Mrs. Horton on the way, the sheriff came around the camper until he was close to where David was lying. "Did you get in the cab before we came?"

"No, sir," David said. "Just partway—through the window."

"Can you tell whether Mr. Horton's pinned or not?"

"His arm may be," David said. "Looks like it's out the window on the other side."

"And the little girl—what about her?"

"Her arm's wedged behind her father, maybe her shoulder's hurt—and her leg's caught somehow."

As if knowing they were talking about her, Jane called in a weak voice, "David—are they getting my mother?"

Before David could answer, Sheriff Tate stood on tiptoe and leaned as close to the window as he could, trying to look inside. "Honey"—his voice was suddenly low and reassuring—"we've got her out—and your little dog—"

"Are they all right?"

David looked at the sheriff, trying to read his thoughts through the dim light, wondering about his expression. "Pup's fine—your mother's shook up a little," Sheriff Tate said, "but she's going to be all right." He glanced at David. "Now we're going to get you and your daddy out."

"Well, please hurry—my arm's hurting. And Daddy—" She let the words trail off.

Sheriff Tate hurried around the front of the camper and aimed his light through the windshield. "Men! Need as many as we can get around this side—we'll use the winch to lift, get the camper on its wheels—"

"Sheriff," David broke in, "they may flop this way."

The sheriff stopped. "You're right—maybe—do you think if you got inside you could brace them?"

"Window's not big enough to crawl through."

"We've got enough men to open the door," the sheriff said, and he called five more to come where he was.

When they were in position, David turned the door latch

and tugged as hard as he could. Once it was an inch open, one man rammed a stick in the crack. Then, crowded together, all of them lifted until they had the door sticking almost straight up. Carefully, David eased himself through the opening and inside.

"What're you doing?" Ronnie yelled.

"He'll be all right," Sheriff Tate answered. "Just getting inside to help get Jane and her father out."

"Well—but don't get caught in that door," Ronnie said.

David locked one leg on the edge of the seat, then felt along the floorboard with his free foot until he found the gearshift hump. He braced himself, and—with flashlight beams through the windshield lighting his way—he squatted on the floor and reached for Mr. Horton's shoulder. "Best I can do!" he yelled out.

"Just hold it there—be fine!" The men let the door down easily; then they and the sheriff backed away. "You men over there—you got the winch hook in place?"

"Got it!" one yelled back.

"Rest of you—grab hold now."

As they ganged around and pressed against the camper body, the cab, and the left front fender, David felt the vehicle shiver. "Donna," the sheriff hollered, "you ready?"

"Ready," she answered. But if she said anything else, David couldn't hear it above the sudden sound of her roaring motor.

He felt the cab lurch as the cable grew taut and the winch began to pull the camper. The sounds of hands slapping and grabbing the lower side sounded like muted drums as the men struggled to help Donna. Once Jane's body shook and she cried out. David was pressing to keep a shifting balance but he moved one hand long enough to touch her shoulder. "Easy—another minute and they'll have it upright."

The effort took longer than David had expected because men now on the upper side were bracing to keep the camper from flopping hard down.

When he felt the right wheels settle and heard the men say, "Got 'er," David relaxed. Partly because he had held them against the seat and partly because Jane was wedged as she was, neither she nor her father had moved more than a few inches from the driver's side.

"How about it, David!"

"They're like they were," he yelled back.

But he did not turn loose until he saw faces through the window on Mr. Horton's side.

"Get that other cot!" the sheriff called. "And if anybody's got a third—"

"Got a sleeping bag and enough men to make a stretcher," somebody said.

Carefully, then, they opened the door on the driver's side, eased Mr. Horton onto the second cot. When they had him moved, Sheriff Tate reached through and gingerly lifted Jane free. A man that David thought he recognized—that's right, Mr. Sam Lennox, had the drug store in Elkton—caught the girl's shoulder and arm and held them from brushing against the cab's side as the sheriff eased her out. They put her on the sleeping bag that was now stretched like a flat surface and carried her around the front of the camper. "Put her in my car—" the sheriff started to say.

"I'll take her in my truck," a man interrupted. "It's covered, got a built-in bed. Somebody can ride back there with her."

"Wait," Jane said. "Is my daddy all right?"

"Honey"—Sheriff Tate touched her hand—"he's going to be okay—broken arm maybe, a bump on his head—but nothing our doctors can't fix."

"Thank you," she said, and her voice was barely above a whisper.

Somebody, David didn't know who, opened the right door once more and he slid out. But by now he was so tired his legs crumpled.

"David!" Ronnie yelled.

"I'll get him!"

David recognized that voice, looked up and wondered when his father had gotten home, wondered what time it was and how long all this had taken. He felt strong, gentle arms lift him.

"Ronnie, get Old Shoe over here."

"Yes, sir."

With help from two other men David didn't know, George Winthrop and Ronnie got him up and onto the saddle. David clutched the saddle horn, shook his head, suddenly aware that the rain wasn't coming down as hard as it had been, felt a hand—had to be his mother's—on his wrist. "Thank God—thank God, David, it's over—"

"Thompson!" Sheriff Tate's yell interrupted her. "Escort these trucks to the hospital—GO!"

George Winthrop caught Old Shoe's bridle and started leading her up the path toward the Ferry Road. Nell Winthrop and Mary Lou joined them. Wasn't the shortest way home but the easiest. As they proceeded, David felt the urge to let his head droop and guessed that Ronnie felt as tired as he was. But wherever he looked, there were people—the men who'd searched the fields, the ones who'd driven along the roads—and all the people who lived in

Rodgersville, he guessed. "George, you've got to be mighty proud of those boys," somebody said.

"Way to go, Ronnie and David." That voice sounded like T. J. Ellis, David couldn't be sure—T.J. was in his grade at school.

Ronnie leaned forward as they rode Old Shoe, with their father guiding them along the way and their mother walking beside him. "Reckon Dad'll be mad about those walkie-talkies and flashlights we lost—you think he'll fuss?" he tried to whisper.

"I heard that," George said softly. "Tomorrow I'm taking you both to Columbus—we'll get the best walkie-talkies and flashlights money can buy."

Ronnie eased back, whispered "Whew," half under his breath.

"Hey, Ronnie, David"—that voice, David knew, had to belong to Shirley Thomkins—"I bet you'll be on radio and TV and in the papers."

David didn't care about radios and TVs and all the newspapers in the world right now. If he could just get to bed and go to sleep—and not dream all night. Just hoped when they got home his father would put Old Shoe in the barn for them—and maybe feed her a little extra because he supposed she was all worn out, too.

ABOUT THE AUTHOR

Hilary Milton (Handle: Railbender) is an active CBer. He has personally been involved in at least fifteen emergencies (10-33s) while operating his Citizens Band radio. He monitored his base continuously for over five hours the night a little boy had been hit by a truck. His daughter, Michelle, became so interested in CB that she is now licensed to broadcast on commercial radio. His wife, Patty, is a writer and he also has a son, David.

This is Hilary Milton's fifth novel. When not writing (which he always does), he teaches at Samford University in his hometown of Birmingham, Alabama.